William Starr Diana

According to season

Talks about the Flowers in the Order of their Appearance in the Woods and Fields

William Starr Diana

According to season
Talks about the Flowers in the Order of their Appearance in the Woods and Fields

ISBN/EAN: 9783337026516

Printed in Europe, USA, Canada, Australia, Japan

Cover: Foto ©Andreas Hilbeck / pixelio.de

More available books at **www.hansebooks.com**

ACCORDING TO SEASON

TALKS ABOUT THE FLOWERS IN
THE ORDER OF THEIR APPEARANCE
IN THE WOODS AND FIELDS

BY

Mrs. William Starr Dana

AUTHOR OF "HOW TO KNOW THE WILD FLOWERS"

"Ah! well I mind the calendar,
Faithful through a thousand years,
Of the painted race of flowers."
—EMERSON

NEW YORK

CHARLES SCRIBNER'S SONS

1894

TROW DIRECTORY
PRINTING AND BOOKBINDING COMPANY
NEW YORK

Preface

*In that the aim of this little volume is the stimula-
tion of an observant love of nature, and especially the increase of knowledge about our plants,
it is similar to "How to Know the Wild Flowers."
But in each book this has been attempted in so
different a mood and manner that I feel confident that neither encroaches upon the province
of the other. The present classification—if a
word so suggestive of technicalities can be used
—is "according to season," and incidentally,
locality, enabling the reader to start upon each
tour of discovery with so clear a notion as to
what he may expect to find, and where he may
expect to find it, as materially to increase the
chances of a successful expedition.*

*Thanks are due to the editor of the Tribune for
permission to republish the articles which appeared in his journal last summer.*

FRANCES THEODORA DANA.

NEW YORK, March 5, 1894.

Table of Contents

PAGE

INTRODUCTORY 1

APRIL AND EARLY MAY 13

MAY AND EARLY JUNE 31

JUNE AND EARLY JULY 47

MIDSUMMER 67

EARLY AUGUST 93

LATE AUGUST AND EARLY SEPTEMBER . 111

AUTUMN 129

INDEX 151

I

Introductory

Self-sown my stately garden grows;
The winds and wind-blown seed,
Cold April rain and colder snows
My hedges plant and feed.

From mountains far and valleys near
The harvests sown to-day
Thrive in all weathers without fear,—
Wild planters, plant away!

—EMERSON.

Behold there in the woods the fine madman . . . .
he accosts the grass and the trees; he feels the blood
of the violet, the clover, and the lily in his veins; and
he talks with the brook that wets his foot.—EMERSON.

I

Introductory

THAT we know so little, as a people, of our birds, trees, rocks and flowers, is not due, I think, so much to any inborn lack of appreciation of the beautiful or interesting, as to the fact that we have been obliged to concentrate our energies in those directions which seemed to lead to some immediate material advantage, leaving us little time to expend upon the study of such objects as promised to yield no tangible remuneration. Then, too, our struggle for existence has taken place largely in towns where there is almost nothing to awaken any dormant love of nature. But, little by little, we are changing all that. Each year a larger portion of our city population is able to seek the refreshment and inspiration of the country during those months when it is almost, if not quite, at its loveliest. And while among this constantly increasing class, there are many, undoubtedly, who "having eyes to see, see not," even among sights sufficiently fraught with interest, one would suppose, to awaken the curiosity of the dullest, yet there are others, many others, who can cry with Mr. Norman Gale,

> "And oh, my heart has understood
> The spider's fragile line of lace,
> The common weed, the woody space !"

who are quick to detect each bird-song, and eager to trace it to its source; who follow curiously the tiny tracks of the wood creatures; who note the varied outlines of the forest leaves, and discover the smallest of the flowers that grows beneath them.

If we do not happen ourselves to be blessed with a natural turn for observation, a little companionship with one of these more fortunate beings will persuade us, I think, that the habit is one which it would be both possible and desirable to cultivate. It had never occurred to me, for example, that it would be worth while to look for wild flowers on Fifth Avenue, until a certain morning when a keen-eyed botanical companion stooped and plucked from an earth-filled chink in its pavement, a little blossom which had found its way hither from some country lane. Since then I have tried to keep my wits about me even on that highway of the Philistines.

We are prone, most of us, to be inaccurate as well as unobservant; and I know of no better antidote to inaccuracy than a faithful study of plants. It is sometimes difficult for the flower-lover to control his impatience when he hears his favorites recklessly miscalled ; and in this improving exercise he has ample opportunity to become proficient, for many people cling with peculiar tenacity and unreasonableness to their first erroneous impression of a flower's name. They consider anything so vague and poetic fair game for their ready imaginations, glibly tacking the name of one flower to another with inconsequential lightheartedness. Occasionally they have really been misled by some similarity of sound. Such was the case of an acquaintance of mine who persisted in informing the various companions of his rambles that the little pink-flowered shrub which blossoms in June on our wooded hillsides was the sheep-sorrel ; and refused to be persuaded that the correct title was sheep - laurel. His ear had caught the words incorrectly ; but although this explanation was suggested, supplemented by the arguments that the laurel - like look of the flowers at once betrayed their lineage, and that the sheep - sorrel was the plant with halberd-shaped leaves and tiny clustered flowers which in spring tinges with red the grassy uplands, he would only reply with dignified decision that his conviction was based on trustworthy authority. So, perhaps, in at least one small circle, sheep-laurel is sheep-sorrel to this day.

But the uninitiated probably allow their imaginations to run more rife with the orchids than with any other flowers. They are usually quite positive as to the general correctness of their conception of an orchid, and unless you are prepared to be made the object of a very genuine aversion, you will beware of trying to convince them of the error of their ways. In response to any such attempt they will defiantly challenge you: " Well, then, what *is* an orchid ? " and woe betide you if you cannot couch your reply in half a dozen words of picturesque and unmistakable description. The term orchid is dear to their hearts. Whenever they discover a rare and striking flower they like to grace it with the title, and are sure to bear you a grudge for depriving them of the pleasurable power of conferring this mark of floral knighthood at will. Last year a friend of mine happened for the first time upon the lovely fringed polygala. Her delight in its butterfly beauty was unbounded. Having learned its name and studied its odd form she turned appealingly to me: "Could you *ever* call it an orchid?" she asked; and I was unpleasantly conscious of my apparent churlishness in refusing to ennoble, even temporarily, so exquisite a creation.

And perhaps it may be explained as well here as elsewhere that to the botanist the chief charm of the orchid lies in its marvellous adaptation to fertilization by insects. Even the schoolboy nowadays is taught that the object of vivid coloring and striking form in a flower is not man's delight, but the production of seed ; in other words, the continuance of the species. He learns that by these means insects are attracted to the nectar-yielding blossoms, and that while rifling them fo their treasure, they inadvertently brush upon their bodies, from the little dust-bags known as anthers, some life-giving pollen which later they are sure to deposit, again unconsciously, upon the moist, roughened disk or stigma of the next flower they visit. Here, the botany teaches, the tiny grains emit tubes which penetrate to the ovules in the ovary below and quicken them into life.

Now it is believed that orchids are peculiarly unfitted to fertilize themselves— that is, if the pollen from the dust bags, or anthers, of any given flower of this family should contrive to reach the moist disk or stigma of that same flower, the chances are that either the little grains would fail to act at all upon the ovules, or that the resultant seeds would lack the vigor so necessary to their survival of the fierce combat in which they are destined to engage. So we observe that the different organs are often so placed that the pollen cannot reach the stigma of its own flower ; and in the orchids especially we find that the most elaborate devices are resorted to in order to attract insect visitors, and to insure the lodgement of the pollen in the right spot. After twenty years of study of the subject, Darwin doubted if he thoroughly understood the contrivances in a single orchid ; so it is not to be wondered that these flowers, even the most inconspicuous among them, invariably awaken eager interest in the student of plant life.

" I like flowers, but I hate to pull

them to pieces," is the cry of the lazy nature-lover. Surely if we like a thing we wish to know something about it, to enjoy some intimacy with it, to learn its secrets. Who actually cares most for flowers, the man who glances admiringly at them and turns away, or he who studies their structure, inquires into the function of each part, reads the meaning of their marvellous coloring, and translates the invitation expressed by their fragrance? I doubt if he who has never been so brutal as "to pull a flower to pieces," even dimly understands all the strange, sweet joy of a wood walk these spring days, when we are tempted eagerly —almost breathlessly—but always reverently, with the reverence that is born of even the beginnings of knowledge, and by so much superior to that which springs from ignorance, to turn the pages and decipher what we can

"In nature's infinite book of secrecy."

When we learn to call the flowers by name we take the first step toward a real intimacy with them. An eager sportsman who had always noticed and wondered about the plants which he met on every fishing expedition, wrote to me a few weeks since that hitherto he had felt toward them as the charity-boy did about the alphabet, "he knew the little beggars by sight, but he couldn't tell their names!" And it has seemed as though a series of papers describing the different flowers to be found in the woods and fields, and by the roadsides, during the months designated in their titles, might not only be helpful to those who care to "tell their names," but might increase the actual number of plants discovered, as one is far more likely to be successful in his search if he has a definite conception of what he can reasonably hope to find.

II

April and Early May

I, country-born an' bred, know where to find
Some blooms thet make the season suit the mind,
An' seem to metch the doubtin' blue-bird's notes,—
Half-vent'rin' liverworts in furry coats,
Bloodroots, whose rolled-up leaves ef you oncurl,
Each on 'em's cradle to a baby-pearl,—
But these are jes' Spring's pickets ; sure ez sin,
The rebble frosts 'll try to drive 'em in ;
For half our May's so awfully like May'nt,
'T would rile a Shaker or an evrige saint ;
Though I own up I like our back'ard springs
That kind o' haggle with their greens an' things,
An' when you 'most give up, 'ithout more words
Toss the field full o' blossoms, leaves, an' birds.

—LOWELL.

II

April and Early May

WINTER excepted, there is only one season when I fail to remind myself of that "least erected spirit" whose

—"looks and thoughts
Were always downward bent;"

for no one who has been ever so faintly touched by the desire to enlarge his circle of plant - acquaintances can deny that he often misses some lovely bit of valley or sky, or even, it may be at times, some distant prospect of surpassing grandeur, because of the eagerness with which he is wont to scrutinize every foot of the immediate wayside. He walks,

15

he rides, he drives, fearful of missing some prize, with watchful eyes "downward bent." I confess to the warmest sympathy with that host or guide whose efforts as cicerone are constantly frustrated by the impatience with which his well-meant expositions are met. It must be exceedingly annoying to have the companion of your drive persist in scanning that side of the road which affords no view, apparently, save that of underbrush, while on the other hand stretch ranges of glorious mountains or peaceful valleys; and simply irritating that the friend whom you have chosen to share with you the beauty of the sunset, say, should inconsiderately interrupt your dissertation upon the quality of the light which is enveloping the hillside, by a disproportionate exclamation of joy as he tears a bedraggled-looking weed from a cleft in the rocks.

No, the would-be botanist can hardly be called companionable, save to himself.

Here, indeed, lies the secret of the charm. He needs no listener to make his rhapsodies satisfying. Every walk abroad is companioned. He rides a hobby which carries him quite as satisfactorily as far more expensive steeds. Less unattainable than a hunter or an indefinite number of polo-ponies, equally it keeps him out of doors, yields him infinite excitement, at times bears him into actual danger, for many a botanist has taken his life into his hands in his search for a coveted specimen. One case of a life's being lost for a flower has come within my personal knowledge. While as a cure for a certain sort of nervousness, I know nothing better than a taste for field botany. A marshy, deep-grown meadow once meant to me only a place to be avoided at all costs, a possible, nay a probable, harborage for the kind of snakes only familiar to me from visits to the Central Park menagerie, the London Zoo, and closely ensuing dreams. The mere thought of venturing across such a tract of land made me shrink with terror; yet to-day the chance of discovering some new orchid, or even a less rare plant, would lead me knee-deep into its midst, without even stopping to consider its slimy possibilities. Once the reaction of disappointment should set in, I own that my retreat might be far from stately.

But I began by saying that during one season only, with the exception of winter, are the eyes of the botanist fixed above more uniformly than below. This is during the early spring, when pretty nearly the only flowers are borne by the trees and shrubs. Ordinarily, these blossoms do not seem to be accredited with any existence at all. I have heard people exclaim with surprise, at the mention of an elm in flower. The city room of a friend of mine looks out upon the spreading branches of a maple. Its occupant takes great pleasure each spring in watching what she calls " the first leaves " unfold themselves; these so-called leaves really being the flowers, very evidently flowers, it would seem, from their brief endurance ; very easily ascertained to be flowers, should a few specimens be gathered for inspection from the thickly strewn pavement below. I remember, too, that when I first planned to write a book about wild flowers, an exceedingly intelligent man asked me if I purposed including " fruit - blossoms." " Fruit-blossoms ? " I asked, sincerely puzzled, not apprehending why one kind of blossoms should be thus designated rather than another, the object of the life of flowers in general being fruit. " Yes ! fruit-blossoms," he repeated impatiently ; " surely you know what *they* are ! " " Frankly, I don't," I answered. " Why, *tree*-blossoms, of course ; apples and pears and peaches and cherries ! "

he explained, evidently supposing, in common, I find, with many others, that "tree-blossoms" were chiefly confined to the domesticated fruit-trees.

We find some of the shrubs flowering even earlier than the trees. During the winter we noticed that the thickets were hung with the scaly catkins of the alders. As spring comes on these catkins swell and soften into tassels of gold and purple ; tassels which are composed of male or staminate flowers, the female or pistillate ones being borne in two or three erect, oblong, cone-like heads.

In hollows still filled with ice and snow, the willows are wearing their soft gray furs. If we break off a branch closely set with the silken "pussies," as the children call them, and place it in a jar of water in the sunshine, the gray soon turns to gold, and the least touch dislodges a yellow cloud of pollen. A shrub which flowers a little later than the early willows is the spice - bush, bearing on its leafless stems close little bunches of pale yellow blossoms which yield an aromatic, faintly penetrating fragrance.

The swamp maple has long been noted for the brilliancy with which it lights the borders of the autumn woods, edging the forest with a flame which daily creeps farther and farther into its midst. It is almost equally noteworthy in April, when from its bare branches burst small clusters of scarlet flowers which show vividly against the cold blue of the spring skies ; and which later, as I remember one year, may fall, like a shower of blood, upon smooth sheets of late snow ; snow which, as it melts, gently uncovers to the sun blue patches of violets. There is a wonderful enchantment about these surprises of the young year. For they are always surprises, never mind how often we have experienced them or how unfailingly we await them. The aroma of the first breath of spring, the concentrated exhalations of the earliest growing things, is fraught with an irresistible intoxication—the intoxication of youth itself.

The silver maple flowers even earlier than its sister of the swamps and low woods, but its yellow or reddish blossoms are less conspicuous. The sugar-maples leaf and flower simultaneously; while the blossoms of the striped and mountain species appear when the trees are in full foliage. With our native elms we find that the blossoms invariably precede the leaves. From the graceful branches of what is perhaps the most beautiful of our trees, the American or white elm, the also yellow or reddish flower-clusters droop from their slender stems in April; while the little, close-set bunches of the slippery, or red, elm may be looked for as early as March.

Like their near of kin, the alders, the

birches have long been hung with the catkins which are now developing into tassels of yellow flowers; the female flowers,
again, as in the alders, being borne in
short, oblong clusters. A little later we
notice the blossoms of the beech, the male
ones drooping in small heads, the female
ones (which later yield the prickly " beech-
nuts ") usually being paired at the tip of
a short stalk.

Although most of these blossoming trees
make little show of brilliancy, relying
largely, I suppose, upon the winds for the
transfer of their pollen, and thus without
inducement to deck themselves as gayly
as would be advisable were they depend-
ent upon the visits of insects, the effect
of their leafless branches festooned with.
slender tassels and tiny flower-clusters is
wonderfully delicate and feathery. Once
appreciated—for these earliest revelations
seem strangely ignored, as though there
were no visible life until the facts of

flower and foliage became conspicuously apparent—their significant beauty is always anticipated with renewed eagerness.

If one looks earthward—where these days the pale sunshine lies with the brooding tenderness of a bird upon its nest, patiently awaiting the life about to burst into being—he sees a multitude of little green cornucopias that are pricking their way upward with a vast deal of determination, undaunted by the matted mass of decaying leaves, failing to be driven back even by the late snowfall. These small objects are so closely " done-up " that they suggest young babies out for their first airing. They have the air of aggressive secrecy peculiar to prize-packets —as if challenging one to guess their contents. And unless our eyes are trained by years of observation, we are indeed quite unable to identify the different plants ; to conjecture that this papery wrapping infolds the pale leaf and pure blossom of the bloodroot; that that vindictive looking spear, composed of closely plaited leaves, heralds the yet remote appearance of the unlovely flowers of the false hellebore; that these slender needles will expand with the feathery foliage and fragile blossoms of the anemone.

But from some last year leaves we are enabled to predict that from certain silken coils will peep the blue eyes of the liverwort. We greet joyfully the familiar evergreen leaves of the trailing arbutus, and when our eager fingers have pushed aside the drifts of dead leaves, we discover a few early, aromatic clusters of its waxen flowers.

Not till the shad-bush flings its white clusters across the brook, does the bloodroot consent to lay aside its wraps and spangle the ground with its snowy gold-centred blossoms. The purity of this flower is only accentuated by the blood-like drops which ooze from its broken stem. A sheltered bank, bright with the young, delicate leaves, and starred with the earlier blossoms of the bloodroot, marks perhaps the loveliest shrine along the path of the ascending year.

By the end of April, and often earlier, the wet meadows look as though tracked with gold. Along the stream, in and out of the swamps, gleam the yellow blossoms of the marsh marigold, a fresh, delightful plant, with tempting leaves, which afford the country people their earliest "greens," and little button-like flower-buds, which make an excellent substitute for capers.

The little blue flowers of the liverwort are not seen at their best until the plant has discarded its worn-out foliage in favor of a fresh set of leaves. But when this renovation has taken place, they are lovely with all the shy suggestiveness peculiar to these early arrivals. In the open woods, among great beds of pale, mottled, pointed leaves, are drooping the lily-like bells of the adder's tongue. Distinctly a rock - loving plant is the Dutchman's breeches, or, more happily named, whitehearts. Sharing some secluded shelf with the evergreen fronds of the polypodium, it enchants us with its delicate foliage, and wands of creamy heart-shaped blossoms. Another rock-frequenting plant, as its title indicates, is the early saxifrage, whose firm, flattish clusters of white flowers, borne at or near the summit of leafless stems, though without the fragile charm of their companions, please us by their wholesome, hearty aspect, and by the impulsive fashion in which they burst from the most unpromising of crannies. Then, too, the saxifrage has a certain finish of its own, one cluster being sufficient unto itself, while, to be appreciated, so many plants need to be seen in the mass; to say nothing of its readiness to be uprooted without "squeaking," and to be carried off without any pretence of swooning by the way. Whoever has struggled with the stubborn tubers of the adder's tongue, tubers which fasten themselves beneath some sharp-edged stone deep in the earth, and has finally conquered its obstinacy only to be foiled by the wilted blossom and drooping leaves, or who has been baffled by the deep-rooted, slender-stemmed tenacity of many other plants, will appreciate the alacrity with which the saxifrage surrenders itself into your keeping, and the absence of any later indication of homesickness.

Where the woods are richer and less rocky, with haughty confidence the wake-robin lifts its three-petalled, purple-red flower. The name of this plant is hardly appropriate, as the woods, nearly a month ago, were alive with robin lovesongs, and by the time it flowers, these birds have begun house-building, if not house-keeping. Beyond, the glen is gay with its kinsmen, the lovely white and painted trilliums. Beneath round, woolly leaves, close to the ground, hide the dingy, cup-shaped blossoms of the wild ginger. From the grass which borders the lane peep the striped stars of the spring-beauty. A little later the overhanging cliff is jewelled with the vivid flowers of the columbine, its curved, spur-like red petals, yellow within; its divided leaves making a soft background of delicate foliage.

But one must keep a tight rein on one's adjectives when describing the early flowers. At this season, not every flower, of course, but pretty nearly every other flower, is possessed of a beauty so unique, so convincing, that for the time being we are forced to yield it unquestioning homage. The delicious aroma and waxen texture of the trailing arbutus, the purity of the bloodroot, the grace of the adder's tongue, the delicacy of the whitehearts, the audacity of the columbine have in turn challenged our allegiance. Yet one is tempted to foreswear one's self anew in favor of the less conspicuous plants. The hillsides are whitened with tremulous anemones. Beneath their leafy arches droop the modest blossoms of the bellwort. At the base of some old oak nestle the soft puff-balls of the dwarf ginseng. And then there are violets, tall, leafy-stemmed yellow violets; low white ones, brown-veined and sweet scented; violets of blue, of lavender, of purple, fringing the brook, and paving the meadow, and flooding the swamp with waves of royal color, always returning to the old, familiar haunts, yet always seeming like new creations of amazing loveliness.

III

May and Early June

The world hangs glittering in star-strown space,
Fresh as a jewel found but yesterday.
                                —T. B. ALDRICH.

III

May and Early June

B Y the roadside the snowy drifts of the dogwood, in the rocky woods the white pyramids of the red-berried elder, along the lane the flat clusters of the early viburnum, give a look of winter past rather than of summer to come. But down in the meadow, great tangles of wild azalea herald the near approach of June, creeping with warm waves of color into every little bay or indentation of the wood.

Into this wood we are tempted by mysterious intervals of light and shade. Beneath cathedral-like arches, with three-divided leaves, and veined, delicately canopied pulpits, quaint Jacks-in-the-pulpit erect themselves. Here the pink bells of the twisted-stalk, and the straw-colored ones of its kinsman, Solomon's seal, are hanging from their curved, leafy stems. Close to the latter, grows its constant companion, the false Solomon's seal, bearing its greenish, somewhat fragrant flowers in a terminal plume, and a near relative (all four belonging to the Lily family), the yet unchristened *Maianthemum*, with one or two smooth green leaves, and a low cluster of whitish flowers. The baneberry and foamflower, too, bear their small white blossoms in soft pyramids at the tips of their stems, the former growing to a height of two feet, and being easily recognized by its divided leaves, those of the latter being heart-shaped and sharply lobed.

Above its pure flower the green umbrellas

of the May-apple are now unfurled. With
each step the tiny blue-veined blossoms
of the speedwell fling us " bon voyage."
More purple than blue are the delicate,
yellow-centred blossoms of the blue-eyed
grass, growing in thick, close tufts. When
the sun is clouded, or if they are picked,
the little blue eyes close tightly and only
the restored sunlight will tempt them to
open again. These are little sisters of
the stately blue flag, which begins to tinge
with rich color the swampy meadows.
" Born to the purple " indeed is the flag,
or fleur-de-lis, full of vigor and self-con-
fidence. I cannot sympathize with Thoreau's assertion that it is " loose and
coarse in its habit," " too showy and
gaudy, like some women's bonnets."

In open sunny places prevail the various shades of yellow. I once heard some
one say that he " couldn't like yellow
flowers, they looked so cheap ! " And
even Wordsworth, ever-faithful celebrant

of the " unassuming commonplace," sings, with poetic inconsistency :

> " Ill befall the yellow flowers,
> Children of the flaring hours ! "

and with little appreciation of the ill which would befall every sunlight-loving eye were his rash wish granted. For who would forego the prodigal gold of the little cinquefoil, which is carpeting every meadow and roadside with those divided leaves which delude so many into the belief that it is a yellow-flowered wild strawberry ? Neither could we spare the glistening blossoms of the common wood-sorrel, whose clover-like leaflets alone serve, with the majority of passers-by, to distinguish it from the cinquefoil. Even the tall, brittle - stemmed, four - petalled celandine, guardian of the village way-side, we would hardly care to be without. Although, perhaps, some of us would cling to it chiefly because we believed it to be identical with the far-famed and much-rhymed "little flower" of Wordsworth, which has never been naturalized in this country and is not even allied to our celandine, a plant of foreign extraction itself.

If any yellow flowers were condemned to banishment, I think we could best spare the Mustards. The winter-cress, or herb of St. Barbara, is the first yellow Mustard to appear, and is so associated with a rubbish heap beyond the wall of some neglected garden, that I doubt if we would regret its disappearance. But even if without sympathy for the Mustards as a family, it is well to learn to recognize them at sight, and this we can usually do by their four white or yellow petals, which are so placed as to form a cross (giving the tribe its Latin name, *Crucifera*), and by the pods, which often appear before all the flowers have passed away.

More attractive than the winter-cress, and plentiful now, is the golden ragwort, suggesting a yellow daisy. In moist places are the flat - topped umbels of the early meadow - parsnip, with yellow, umbrella - like clusters which betray their kinship with the white wild carrot of summer, and the origin of the scientific name of their family, *Umbelliferæ*.

Certain meadows are flooded with deep orange. If we explore their depths we discover the smooth, slender stems, pale leaves, and deep-hued flower-heads (suggesting dandelions somewhat) of the cynthia. Great patches of these are interspersed with lavender masses of wild geranium, a flower nearly allied to the blossom which led the German student, Sprengel, to suspect the important ministrations of insects to plants. He pondered long the significance of the bearded throat which protects the nectar from rain and useless insects, convinced that "the wise author of nature had not created a hair in vain."

These flowers are sometimes spoken of as blue, again as pink, again as purple, but I believe the majority will agree that "pink-purple" best describes their radiant hue. Soon the five rounded petals will fall, revealing a beak - like projection, which will enlarge until finally it splits apart into five separate pieces, with such force as to project the tiny seeds within to some distance; thus affording them a better chance of securing a desirable foothold than if they were all allowed to fall directly beneath the parent plant. This beak-like object accounts for the title, "wild cranesbill," which the flower sometimes bears.

There are some few plants, the discovery of which makes the day especially memorable. Among these is the twin-flower, or *Linnæa*, the lovely

> —"monument of the man of flowers,
> Which breathes his sweet fame through the
> northern bowers."

It is not easy to forget the moment when, in the depth of the lonely wood, we become suddenly conscious of a delicious fragrance, and our eyes fall for the first time upon a carpet of tiny, rounded leaves, and thread - like, forking stems which are hung with the pink sister-blossoms. Another May flower whose first finding is a delight, is the little fringed polygala. Its foliage is so delicate, its pink-purple blossoms so butterfly-like in their beauty.

The discovery of an orchid is always an occasion. The first to appear is the showy orchis, with its two oblong, shining leaves, and loose spike of purple-pink, white-lipped flowers.

Not much later is the Indian moccason, or lady's slipper. This plant is to me especially suggestive of the wilder woods. When we find its striped pink pouch swinging from a stout stem between two large veiny leaves, it looks as though it were guarding some mysterious secret. It was almost a disappointment last year to come across a whole flock of these flowers beneath the pines which skirted a neighbor's lawn. When an orchid leaves its exclusive haunts for a gentleman's country seat we feel a little as if a queen had stepped from her throne to mingle promiscuously with her subjects. I doubt if either of the yellow species would so demean themselves. One should soon begin to search well the wooded hillsides if he wish to possess himself of the bright beauty of " whip-poor-will's shoe," as the larger yellow lady's slipper is sometimes called, and the lonely swamps if he hope for the smaller, more fragrant variety.

In the deep rich woods where we find the twin-flowers are masses of the dark, shining foliage and straw-colored blossoms of the *Clintonia*. Thick in our path lie the three-divided leaves and tiny flowers of the gold-thread, and we stoop to pluck from the moist, dark earth, a handful of its bright yellow roots.

Just here the ground begins to yield beneath us, and we find ourselves on the edge of an open marsh, which is closely skirted, on every side, by tall trees. Intense quiet reigns — only broken by the occasional croaking of a frog, or some distant bird-note. The rushes grow tall and green. Coronet-like clusters of the beautiful royal fern, *Osmunda regalis*, lift themselves to a height of several feet, their delicate central fronds tipped with clusters of greenish fruit. Here, too, are great circles of the cinnamon-fern, another *Osmunda*, its golden-brown fruiting fronds set amid a mass of rich foliage.

Our feet sink deep in the spongy sphagnum, but we pay little heed to the warning, for tall spikes of pale lilac, deeply fringed flowers meet our expectant eyes, and we know that at last our long search for the great purple - fringed orchis is crowned with success. Through many a mosquito-ridden marsh have we floundered in its vain quest, but perhaps now we only prize it the more for our long probation.

Some one has said that the swamp is nature's sanctuary. Truly, such a remote, hushed, luxuriant spot as this, so full of her rarer beauties, free from any suggestion of man, seems almost like her " holy of holies," and we feel as if we had been somewhat intrusive in our reckless search after loveliness.

But all such hyper - sensitiveness vanishes as we perceive a great, snowy patch on the farther side of the marsh. Regardless of their lace-like clusters we push our way through thickets of dogwood and viburnum, rudely shake the pink blossoms from the wild azalea which bars our way, tread underfoot the rank leaves of skunk-cabbage and false hellebore, and, with shoes filled with water to their utmost capacity, we reach finally masses of the funnel-shaped, white-bearded flowers of the buckbean.

Near at hand we excitedly espy the "brimming beakers" of the pitcher-plant —winged, hooded leaves relentlessly holding captive a host of unfortunate insects, which have been tempted into their hollows by the sugary exudation for which they have unwittingly bartered their lives —for the downward pointing bristles will prevent their escape. The plant is said to be nourished by the decomposing bodies of these captives, and we fancy that the great, purple-red flowers which nod from their tall stalks have drawn their hue and vigor from the blood of a hundred victims.

Our homeward way leads us through pastures reddened with sheep - sorrel, gemmed with the yellow constellations of the stargrass, and enamelled with delicate bluets, or Quaker-ladies. As we cross a stream bordered with forget-me-nots, we reach a meadow riotous with the lavish beauty of the wild lupine, whose long, bright clusters of pea-like blossoms make the hillside seem a reflection of June skies.

Buttercups and daisies are opening their " golden eyes " and taking their first look at the new year. But despite the exquisite freshness which so generally prevails, speaking of promise rather than accomplishment—which is the beginning of the end—the berries of the shadbush have begun to crimson in the thicket, and along the footpath gleam the silver fruit-spheres of the dandelion.

IV

June and Early July

Now is the high-tide of the year,
And whatever of life hath ebbed away
Comes flooding back with a ripply cheer
Into every bare inlet and creek and bay.
—LOWELL.

IV

June and Early July

WHEN Coleridge called this

—" the leafy month of June "

it seems to me that he struck
the note of the first summer month more
distinctly than our own Bryant, who wrote
of " flowery June." June is, above all
things, " leafy," seeming chiefly to concentrate her energies on her foliage ; for
although she really is not lacking in flowers, they are almost swamped in the great
green flood which has swept silently but
irresistibly across the land. At times one
loses sight of them altogether, and fan-

cies that a sort of reaction has set in after

—" festival
Of breaking bud and scented breath,"

that which enchained our senses a few weeks since.

But the sight of a clover - field alone suffices to dispel the thought. There is no suggestion of exhaustion in the close, sweet - scented, wholesome heads which are nodding over whole acres of land.

" South winds jostle them,
    Bumblebees come,
    Hover, hesitate,
    Drink and are gone,"

sings Emily Dickinson, who elsewhere calls the clover the

—" flower that bees prefer
And butterflies desire."

Indeed, although this is not a native blossom, it seems to have taken a special hold on the imaginations of our poets. Mr. James Whitcomb Riley asks,

> —" what is the lily and all of the rest
> Of the flowers to a man with a heart in his breast
> That was dipped brimmin' full of the honey and dew
> Of the sweet clover blossoms his babyhood knew ? "

It is generally acknowledged that our sense of smell is so intimately connected with our powers of memory that odors serve to recall, with peculiar vividness, the particular scenes with which they are associated. Many of us have been startled by some swiftly borne, perhaps unrecognized, fragrance, which, for a brief instant, has forcibly projected us into the past; and I can imagine that a sensitively organized individual — and surely the poet is the outcome of a peculiarly sensitive and highly developed organization — might be carried back, with the strong scent of the clover field, to the days when its breath was a sufficient joy, and its limits barred out all possibility of disaster.

If we pluck from the rounded heads one tiny flower and examine it with a magnifying glass we see that it has somewhat the butterfly shape of its kinsman, the sweet - pea of the garden. We remember that as children we followed the bee's example and sucked from its slender tube the nectar ; and we conclude that the combined presence of irregularity of form, nectar, vivid coloring, and fragrance indicate a need of insect visitors for the exchange of pollen and consequent setting of seed, as Nature never expends so much effort without some clear end in view.

As an instance of the strange ''web of complex relations,'' to quote Darwin, which binds together the various forms of life, I recall a statement, which created some amusement at a meeting of the English Royal Agricultural Society, to the effect that the growth of pink clover depended largely on the proximity of old women. The speaker argued that old women kept cats ; cats killed mice ; mice were prone to destroy the nests of the bumblebees, which alone were fitted, owing to the length of their probosces, to fertilize the blossoms of the clover. Consequently, a good supply of clover depended on an abundance of old women.

The little yellow hop-clover has just begun to make its appearance in the sandy fields and along the roadsides. Although it is very common, and in spite of its general resemblance, both in leaf and flower, to the other clovers, it seems to be recognized but seldom. I have known people to gather it with unction and send it to some distant botanical friend as a rarity.

One morning last fall I found a quantity of blood-red clover - heads by the

roadside. As I was gathering a few—
never before having seen this species, I
was confident—a woman came out from
the neighboring farm-house to tell me that
her husband had planted his clover-seed,
as usual, the previous spring, and had
been much amazed at the appearance of
this flaming crop. She was eager to
know if I could tell her what sort of
clover it was that yielded these unusual
blossoms.

A careful search through my '' Gray ''
left me quite in the dark. Every plant-
lover knows the sense of defeat that comes
with the acknowledgment that you cannot place a flower, and will sympathize
with the satisfaction which I experienced
a few days later when, while reading in
- one of Mr. Burroughs's books an account
of a country walk in England, I found a
description of *Trifolium incarnatum*, a
clover common on the other side but almost unknown here, that exactly tallied

with the appearance of the recently discovered stranger, which by some chance
had found its way to the dooryard of the
Connecticut farmer.

Except for the arrival of the clovers
and for the constant reinforcement in the
ranks of daisies and buttercups, the appearance of the fields has not altered
greatly during the last two weeks. Blue
flags still lift their stately heads along the
water-courses, and the blossoms of the
blue-eyed grass are now so large and
abundant that they seem to float like a
flood of color on the tops of the long
grasses. I do not remember ever to have
seen these flowers so vigorous and conspicuous as they are this year. In the
wet meadows, at least, the blues now predominate, rather than the yellows. Almost the only yellow flower that is at all
abundant among the flags and blue eyes
is a day-blooming species of the evening primrose, with delicate, four-petalled

flowers scattered about the upper part of the slender stems.

It is Richard Jefferies who finds fault with the artists for the profuseness with which they scattered flowers upon their canvases; but, for myself, I recall no painted meadow more thickly strewn with blossoms than the actual one which stretches before me. It seems to me that the fault to-day lies more in the quality of the painting than in the quantity of the flowers.

It is in the face of modern tradition that one wishes to see these indicated with some fidelity and tenderness; yet I cannot but feel that the old Italians— Fra Angelico, for example—caught better the spirit of the fields of Paradise when he starred them with separate, gemlike flowers, than do our modern men that of our own meadows, which they dash with reckless splashes of color, expecting the leafless, stemless blotches to

do duty for the most exquisitely tinted .
and delicately modelled of Nature's prod-
ucts. And I think that one recalls more
vividly in the galleries of Florence than
in those of Fifty-seventh Street the near
effect of the flower-spangled fields which
border our Hudson.

Bounding one favorite meadow is a
row of tall elms, and a winding, shadowy
thicket. Here red - winged blackbirds
flash in and out: song-sparrows give vent
to their inexhaustible joy in life; and
the restless brown thrasher catches the
sunlight on its tawny coat. Just such a
neighborhood is sure to tempt one away
from the frank loveliness of the open fields
for the mere possibilities of — I hardly
know what. Perhaps some low-built nest
with its cluster of bluish-green, or white,
brown-flecked eggs, guarded by the anx-
ious mother-bird, whose high, terrified
notes we fancy we recognize as we approach. Or perhaps one of the rarer or-

chids is hidden among the rushes beyond.

It is hardly too early to look for the showy lady's slipper, loveliest of a lovely tribe. For an instant a group of tall stems and veiny leaves mislead us by their likeness to those of the ladies' slippers, and we look eagerly for the large white and purple pouch, only to discover the deception when we notice the ugly, greenish flowers of the false hellebore. We are more likely to be successful in our orchid hunt if we are less ambitious—if we are willing to content ourselves with the two oblong shining leaves and the low purplish clusters of the twayblade, or with the long, dull spikes of the green orchis.

A grassy lane promises to lead to some distant woods. The wild grape flings its graceful festoons overhead. The air is heavy with the sweet-scented breath of its greenish flowers. Against the rail fence viburnums grow tall and thick, with toothed, bright green leaves heavily veined on the under side, and flat clusters of white flowers on which are huddled little groups of sleepy fireflies. In and out twist the prickly stems, shining, decorative leaves and greenish blossoms of the cat-brier. The carrion-vine, too, sends forth its delicate young shoots, but the foul odor of its dull clustered blossoms, which has attracted all the carrion-liking flies in the neighborhood, drives us hurriedly from its vicinity.

About the trunks and close branches of slim cedars twine the strong stems and rich, glossy leaves of the poison-ivy. If we are wise we tarry here no longer than by the carrion-vine, for the small white flowers, which are now fully open, are said to give forth peculiarly poisonous emanations under the influence of the June sun.

In the woods the maple-like leaves and white flowers of the laurestinus, or maple-leaved viburnum, are noticeable. In places the ground is white with the pretty dwarf cornel or bunch-berry. Each low stem is crowned with four large white, or pink-tipped, petal-like leaves, which surround a cluster of tiny greenish flowers; from four to six oblong, pointed, green leaves are crowded in a circle below. This is the small sister of the well-known dogwood which so lately seemed to link June with January.

The shrubby dogwoods, some of which are still blossoming along the roadsides, bear a superficial resemblance to the viburnums; but their tiny flowers are minutely four-toothed, while those of the viburnums are five-lobed. Among fallen, moss-grown trunks we find the clover-like leaflets (resembling those of the common yellow wood-sorrel) and the white, pink-veined flowers of the wood-sorrel.

Along the sheltered roadside, as well as in the woods, the delicate white bells of the pyrola droop from their slender stem in a fashion which suggests the lily-of-the-valley. The long, curved pistil which protrudes from each flower easily distinguishes this plant from the pipsissewa, which can also be recognized by its glossy, evergreen, occasionally white-veined leaves, and by its fragrant waxen flowers with violet-colored anthers.

Although the pyrola and pipsissewa are sometimes found growing together, the former usually requires a rather moist, rich soil, while the latter flourishes best in sandy places among decaying leaves. The pyrola is the first of the two to blossom, and its flowers can soon be found in great abundance, while those of the pipsissewa are hardly in their prime till July. With their disappearance I feel as if the curtain had been rung down upon the host of shy, lovely wood flowers of the early year. The later arrivals, in spite of their usual beauty and vigor, lack the timid grace which we rarely miss in the earlier ones.

On the rocky hillsides the glory of the mountain - laurel is at its height. The wood openings reveal what look like drifts of snow—the snow of the Alps by dawn or early twilight—for in sunny places the flowers of this laurel are pure rose-color, although in the deeper woods they are white. The thick, glossy leaves form an effective background to the dense clusters of wholesome - looking flowers. Perhaps the firm, fluted, pink-tinged buds are even prettier than the blossoms. Pick a freshly opened cluster and observe that each of the ten little bags of pollen is caught in a separate de-pression of the wheel - shaped corolla. Brush the flower, lightly but quickly, with your finger or a twig, and you see that the bags are dislodged by the jar with such force that your finger is thickly dusted with pollen, and you understand how the visiting bee unconsciously transmits the precious grains from flower to flower.

Strictly speaking, the waxy flowers of the rhododendron are more beautiful than those of the laurel, but in our latitude the rhododendron is not only far less abundant, but also far less luxuriant in growth and foliage. Thoreau is tireless in his admiration of the "small, ten-sided, rosy - crimson basins" of the sheep - laurel, or lamb-kill, a low shrub with pale green, narrowly oblong leaves, and flowers which resemble, except in size and color, those of the mountain laurel, in whose immediate neighborhood they are found.

Not far from the laurels we find the Indian cucumber-root, with small, yellowish flowers drooping from slender, woolclad stems, above a circle of oblong pointed leaves. This delicate little plant is less effective now than in September, when its clustered purple berries and brilliantly painted leaves are sure to detain the eye. Its tuberous root, with a strong flavor of the cucumber, was very probably used as food by the Indians.

Even in midwinter we can go to the woods, and, brushing away the snow from about the roots of some old tree, find the shining white-veined leaves and coral - like berries of the partridge - vine. But this is the season when we should make a special pilgrimage to some dim retreat which is pervaded with the fragrance of its lovely white and pinkish twin-blossoms.

So frequent and enchanting are the revelations which await us these days that, to the man or woman with unburdened mind and enlightened vision, a country ramble is one of the most perfect of pleasures. Then there are days when the odor-laden winds seem to have some narcotic power, lulling to inertia all energy and ambition; days when the drowsily witnessed voyage of a butterfly, or the half-heard song of a wood-thrush, or even the dreamy consciousness of the rhythmical development of life about us —the measured succession of bud, flower, and fruit—seems a sufficient end in itself.

It is easier to resist this influence if we keep to the road. Once we are led away by some winding pretence of a path, each leafy curve of which is more enticing than the last, we are apt to yield ourselves to the simple charm of being. But on the road we are more practical, more self-conscious. We only cease entirely to be self-conscious when there is no chance of human interruption. On the road a farm-wagon may overtake us at any moment, and we feel that, to the bovine mind, even the foolish occupation of picking flowers seems more intelligent than the abandonment of one's self to joy in the blue of the sky or the breath of summer.

Flat rosettes of purple - veined leaves and tall clusters of dandelion-like flower-heads abound by the dusty highway. The striped leaves suggested the markings of the rattlesnake to some imaginative mind : and so the plant has been dubbed "rattlesnake weed," and the superstitious have used it as the cure for the bites of the rattlesnake. Narrow leaves and pretty, spotted flowers on hair-like stalks grow in many circles about the slender stems of the yellow loosestrife.

The blackberry vines are less white than they were ten days ago, and hard, green berries are replacing the flowers. The slender, light blue clusters of the larger skull-cap are beginning to be noticeable. Through the grasses glistens the wet scarlet of wild strawberries. In the thicket are shrubs, whose green buds are still too firmly closed for us to guess their names, unless we chance to recognize their leaves. There is always something to look forward to—something to come back for—even along the roadside.

V

Midsummer

Or else perhaps I sought some meadow low,
Where deep-fringed orchids reared their feathery spires,
   Where lilies nodded by the river slow,
   And milkweeds burned their red and orange fires ;
Where bright-winged blackbirds flashed like living
      coals,
   And reed-birds fluted from the swaying grass :
   There shared I in the laden bee's delight,
   Quivered to see the dark cloud-shadows pass
   Beyond me ; loved and yearned to know the souls
   Of bird and bee and flower—of day and night.

V

Midsummer

IT is interesting to observe the manner in which the flowers express the dominant mood of the season. The early ones, as has been noticed already, are chilly-looking, shy, tentative ; charming with the shrinking, uncertain charm of an American spring. Those of the later year are distinctly hardy, braced to meet cold winds and nipping nights. While those of midsummer—those which are abroad now—have caught the hot look of flame, or of the sun itself, or—at times—the deep blue of the sky.

Of course there are exceptions to this

rule, as we shall note later ; but the least observing must admit the intensity of the colors which now prevail, colors which are not perhaps more brilliant than the later ones, but which, it seems to me, are far more suggestive of summer. It may be argued that this is merely a matter of association ; that if the golden-rods and asters were in the habit of flowering in July, and if the lilies and milkweeds ordinarily postponed their appearance till September, the former would seem to us the ones which embodied most vividly the idea of heat and sunlight, while the latter would typify, in a perfectly satisfactory fashion, the colder season.

I am ready to acknowledge that we are victimized sometimes by our sensitiveness to association ; recalling clearly a certain childish conviction that one could recognize Sunday by the peculiarly golden look of its sunlight, and by the long, mysterious slant of its shadows in the orchard. This delusion—though even yet it hardly seems that—sprang, I suppose, partly from the façt that only on Sunday was one obliged to refrain from a variety of enchanting pursuits which at other times proved so absorbing as to preclude any great sensitiveness to the aspects of nature, and partly also from a certain serenity in the moral atmosphere which so linked itself with the visible surroundings as to arouse the belief that the lights and shadows of this one day actually differed in character from those of the other six. Still I cannot but think that not only is the coarseness of habit common to the later flowers suggestive of a defensive attitude in view of a more or less inclement season, but that their actual colors are less indicative of the heat of summer.

Surely no autumn field sends upward a multiple reflection of the sun itself as do these meadows about us. One would

suppose that the yellow rays of the omnipresent black-eyed Susan would droop
beneath the fierce ones which beat upon
them from above. Instead, they seem to
welcome the touch of a kinsman and to
gain vigor from the contact. One instantly recognizes these flowers as members of the great Composite family, a
tribe which is beginning to take almost
undisputed possession of many of our
fields ; that is, in relation to the floral
world, for the farmers are waging constant war upon it. They are cousins of
the dandelions and daisies, of the golden-
rod and asters.

The family name indicates that each
flower-head is composed of a number of
small flowers which are clustered so closely as to give the effect of a single blossom. In the black-eyed Susan the brown
centre, the " black eye " itself, consists of
a quantity of tubular - shaped blossoms,
which are crowded upon a somewhat

cone-shaped receptacle, hence the common name of "cone-flower." In botanical parlance, these are called "disk flowers." They possess both stamens and pistils, while the yellow rays, which commonly are regarded as petals, are in reality flowers which are without either of these important organs; only assisting in the perpetuation of the species by arresting the attention of passing insects and thus securing an exchange of pollen among the perfect disk-flowers.

In the common daisy the arrangement is different. Here the white rays are even more useful than ornamental, as they are the female flowers of the head, eventually producing seed; while the yellow disk-flowers of the centre yield the pollen. The dandelion is without any tubular blossoms. Its florets are botanically described as "strap-shaped," resembling the ray-flowers of the daisy and black-eyed Susan. In the common thistle, again, we find only tubular flowers. If the minute blossoms of the Composite family were not thus grouped, probably they would be too inconspicuous to attract attention and often might fail to secure the pollen necessary to their fertilization. To quote Mr. Grant Allen, " Union is strength for the daisy as for the State."

More people would learn to take an interest in plants if they suspected the pleasurable excitement which awaits the flower-lover upon the most commonplace railway journey. A peculiar thrill of expectancy is caused by the rapidly changing environment which reveals, in swift succession, flowers of the most varied proclivities. If we leave New York on a certain road, at intervals for an hour or more the salt marshes spread their deep-hued treasures before us. Then we turn into the interior, passing through farmlands where the plants which follow in the wake of civilization line our way. Suddenly we leave these behind. Darting into the deep forest we catch glimpses of the shyer woodland beauties. Now and then we span a foaming river, on whose steep shores we may detect, with the eagerness of a sportsman, some long-sought rarity.

It is always a fresh surprise and disappointment to me to find that I can seldom reach on foot such wild and promising spots as the railway window reveals. Is it possible that the swiftly vanishing scene has been illuminated by the imagination which has been allowed the freer play from the improbability of any necessity for future readjustment? However that may be, I find that my book possesses but little charm till an aching head warns me to refrain from too constant a vigil.

Just now, from such a coigne of vantage, when the unclouded sun beats upon their surfaces, certain pastures look as though afire. The grasses sway about great patches of intense orange-red, suggestive of creeping flames. This startling effect is given by the butterfly-weed, the most gorgeous member of the milkweed family. Almost equally vivid, though less flame-like, is the purple milkweed, a species which abounds also in dry places, with deep pink-purple flowers which grow in smaller, less spreading clusters than those of the butterfly-weed. The swamp milkweed may be found in nearly all wet meadows. It is described by Gray as "rose-purple," but the finer specimens might almost claim to be ranked among the red flowers.

The dull pink balls of the common milkweed or silkweed are massed by every roadside now, and are too generally known to need description. The most delicate member of the family is the four-leaved milkweed, with fragrant pale pink blossoms which appear in June on the wooded hillsides. Although there are eighteen distinct species of milkweed proper, perhaps the above are the only ones which are commonly encountered. Few plant-families add more to the beauty of the summer fields. But although its different representatives are deemed worthy of careful cultivation in other countries—the well-known swallow-worts of English gardens being milkweeds—I doubt if the average American knows even the commoner species by sight, so careless have we been of our native flowers.

July yields no plant which is more perfect in both flower and foliage than the meadow lily. It is a genuine delight to wade knee-deep into some meadow among the myriad erect stems, which are surrounded by symmetrical circles of lance-shaped leaves and crowned with long-stemmed, nodding, recurved lilies ; lilies so bell - like and tremulous that such a meadow always suggests to me possibilities of tinkling music too ethereal for mortal ears. Usually these flowers are yellow, thickly spotted with brown, but this year I find them of the deepest shade of orange. Within the flower-cup the stamens are heavily loaded with brown pollen.

When with rhythmical sweep of his long scythe the mower lays low whole acres of lilies and clover, milkweeds, daisies, and buttercups, there is a tendency to bewail such a massacre of the flowers. But, after all, this is no purposeless destruction. As the dead blossoms lie heaped one upon another in the blazing sunlight, their sweetness is scattered abroad with every breath of wind. As we rest among the fragrant mounds we are still subject to their pervading influence. They " were lovely and pleasant in their lives, and in their death they were not divided."

But it is not the sentimentalist only

who begrudges every flower that is picked
without purpose, to be thrown aside, a
repulsive, disfigured object, a few mo-
ments later. Certainly it seems unintel-
ligent, if not wasteful and irreverent, to
be possessed with an irresistible desire
wantonly to destroy an exquisite organ-
ism. Yet so frequent is this form of un-
intelligence that when the companioned
flower-lover discovers a group of what he
fears might be considered tempting blossoms, his instinct is to pounce upon them
with outstretched arms and protect them
from an almost certain onslaught.

Thoreau says somewhere that life should
be lived "as tenderly and daintily as one
would pluck a flower," so it is possible
that in the neighborhood of Walden the
ruthless flower-gatherers were in the mi-
nority, for one would regret to see a life
lived as roughly and without semblance of
daintiness as one see, in less fortunate localities, flowers plucked by the dozen.

In the woods and along the thicket-bordered fields the vivid cups of the wood lily gleam from clusters of dull bracken or from feathery, gold - tinged fern-beds. These had never seemed to me so almost blood-like in color as when I caught constant glimpses of them from the train a few days ago. As it had been raining heavily, I thought that the unusual intensity of their hue might be due to a recent bath. But in my wanderings since then I have encountered equally brilliant specimens, and again conclude that the flowers of this year are unusually deep-hued and vigorous.

The Turk's cap lily, the well-named *Lilium superbum* of the botanies, is nearly always so imposing — with its stout stem, that, at its best, would overtop a giant, and with its radiant, recurved flowers, thirty or forty of which are sometimes found on one plant—that it is almost sure to surprise us anew whenever

we rediscover it. It is found in rich,
low ground, reaching great perfection in
some of the swampy places near the Connecticut shore of Long Island Sound.
It resembles somewhat the tiger - lily,
which was brought to us from Asia, and
which has escaped in hosts to the roadside and marks the site of many a de-
serted homestead.

However much we may revel in rich
color, it is restful, after a time, to turn
from these blazing children of the sun to
the green water-courses which are marked
by the white, pyramidal clusters and
graceful foliage of the tall meadow-rue.
On certain of these plants the flowers are
exquisitely delicate and feathery, while
on others they are comparatively coarse
and dull. A closer inspection reveals
that the former are the male, the latter
the female flowers.

This distinction between the sexes, however, is less marked in the world of flow-

ers than in that of birds. During the past week I have watched the comings and goings of a scarlet tanager, which had built his nest in the fork of a pine-tree within easy view of my window, and have had ample opportunity to contrast the tropical brilliancy of his plumage with the dull greenish dress of his mate, a contrast greater than any I have noticed among similarly related flowers.

Almost as refreshing as the masses of meadow-rue are the thickets composed of the deep green leaves and white, spreading flowers of the elder. Another beautiful shrub, which is now blossoming in marshy places, especially near the coast, is the fragrant white swamp honeysuckle. Only among the sandhills of the coast itself do we meet with the purplish blossoms of the beach-pea. Nearly akin to it is the blue vetch, whose long, dense, one-sided clusters of small pea-like flow-crs make little lakes of pinkish blue in wet meadows farther inland.

Although still unsuccessful in my search for the home of the showy lady's slipper, the appearance of whose leaf and stem the false hellebore simulated so successfully a month ago, I have at last seen, by a fortunate chance, this rarely beautiful flower. A country boy, whose identity as yet I have been unable to discover, left at my door a bunch of the great beauties, and I have revelled in their full, shell-like, pink-striped lips, their white, spreading petals and their delicious fragrance. "Peat-bogs, Maine to North Carolina, July," hardly indicates the many hours which, if one experience goes for anything, must be spent in their quest.

Less difficult of attainment is the grass-pink, or *Calopogon*. This is the only orchid, I believe, which carries its lip on the upper instead of on the lower side of the flower, a contrast to the usual arrangement which is owing to the non-twisting of the ovary. The deep pink flowers, with their spreading white, yellow, and pink-bearded lips, are clustered near the summit of a stem which is about a foot high. The single leaf is long and narrow.

In the same bog which yields the grass-pinks in abundance, I find also the lovely rose - colored, violet - scented adder's mouth, the long, uninteresting spikes of the green orchis, and the white fragrant wands of the northern white orchis. From now till August a careful search of any wet meadow may discover the closely spiked, sweet - scented flowers of another not infrequent member of the family, the smaller of the purple-fringed orchises.

In the dry woods we encounter constantly a shrubby plant with rounded clusters of small white flowers. This is the New Jersey tea, or red-root; the former name arising from the use made of its leaves during the Revolution, the latter from its dark red root. The driest and most uninviting localities do not seem to discourage either this persistent little shrub or the bushy-looking wild indigo, with its clover-like leaves and short terminal clusters of yellow, pea-like blossoms.

In shaded hollows and on the hillsides the tall white wands of the black cohosh, or bugbane, shoot upward, rocket-like. The great stout stems, large divided leaves and slender spikes of feathery flowers render this the most conspicuous wood plant of the season. If we chance to be lingering

" In secret paths that thread the forest land "

when the last sunlight has died away, and happen suddenly upon one of these ghostly groups, the effect is almost startling. The rank odor of the flowers detracts somewhat from one's enjoyment of their beauty, and is responsible, I suppose, for their unpleasing title of bugbane.

Under the pine-trees are the glossy leaves and nodding bells of the winter-green ; while here and there spring grace-ful, wax-like clusters of parasitic Indian pipe, the fresh blossoms nodding from leafless, fleshy stalks, the older ones erecting themselves preparatory to fruit-ing. When we pick these odd-looking flowers they turn black from our touch, adding their protest to the cry against the despoiler, and invalidating their claim to the title which they sometimes bear of "corpse-plant."

From some deep shadow gleam the coral-like berries of the early elder, or the bright, rigid clusters of the bane-berry. On the low bush - honeysuckle the deeper-colored yellow blossoms an-nounce to the insect world that they have no attractions to offer in the way of pollen or honey, their fertilization be-ing achieved already.

But at present the woods are not altogether satisfactory hunting grounds. The more interesting flowers have sought the combined light and moisture of the open bogs or the sunshine of the fields and roadsides. Along the latter are quantities of bladder-campion, a European member of the Pink family which has established itself in Eastern New England. It can be recognized at once by its much-inflated calyx and by its deeply parted white petals. A few days since I found the wayside whitened with the large flowers of the lovely summer anemone, each one springing from between two closely set, deeply cut leaves, in the distance suggesting white wild geraniums. A near kinsman, the thimble - weed, is apt to be confused with the summer anemone when it is found bearing white instead of greenish flowers. This curious-looking plant is noticeable now in shaded spots, growing to a height of two or three feet, and sending up gaunt flower-stalks which are finally crowned with a large, oblong, thimble-like head of fruit.

Banked in hollows of the hillside are tall, nodding wands of willow - herb or fire-weed, with delicate flowers of intense purple - pink. Each blossom contains both stamens and pistil, but these mature at different times, and so-called "self-fertilization" is prevented. The pollen is discharged from the stamens while the immature pistil is still bent backward, with its stigmas so closed as to render it impossible for them to receive upon their surfaces a single quickening grain. Later it erects itself, spreading its four stigmas, which now secure easily any pollen which may have been brushed upon the body of the visiting bee. These flowers are so large and are visited so constantly by bees that any one who chances upon the plant can witness speedily the whole performance.

Here are raspberry bushes covered

thickly with fruit, so thickly that one could live for days on the rocky hillside without other food than this most subtly flavored of all berries. Overhead its purple-flowered sister betrays its kinship with the now abundant wild rose, whose delicate beauty it fails utterly to rival. In the low thicket are tiny, rose-veined bells of dogbane, and beyond, the bright if somewhat ragged, yellow flowers and dotted leaves of the irrepressible St. John's-wort jut up everywhere.

The umbrella-like clusters of the water hemlock fill the moist ditches and suggest the wild carrot of the later year ; close by the coarse stems and flat, yellow tops of its relative, the meadow parsnip, crowd one upon another. Farther on are soft plumes of the later yellow loosestrife, with little flowers similar to those of the four-leaved loosestrife, which is now on the wane.

One looks down upon a wood from

whose edges gleam silvery birches, whose tops are soft with the tassels of the chestnut. Below it slopes a meadow turned yellow with the pale flowers of the wild radish. Above it surges a field of grain which grows dark and cool with the shadow of a scurrying cloud. If one were nearer he would see among the wheat the bright pink - purple petals and green ruff - like calyx of the corn cockle.

The year is at its height. The bosom of the earth is soft and restful as that of a mother. One abides in its perfect present, looking neither behind nor before. With the ever-recurring scent of new-mown hay comes another odor, aromatic, permeating. From our feet slopes

" —a bank where the wild thyme grows."

Only in this one spot have I ever met with this classic little plant, with its close purple flowers and tiny rigid leaves.

When I first discovered it, one superb
rain-washed afternoon, the line

> "From dewy pastures, uplands sweet with
> thyme,"

from Mr. Watson's poem on Wordsworth,
flashed into my mind, and for the hun-
dredth time I appreciated the humor of
Mr. Oscar Wilde's assertion to the effect
that the chief use of Nature is to illus-
trate quotations from the poets.

VI

Early August

It seems as if the day was not wholly profane in which we have given heed to some natural object.

—Emerson.

VI

Early August

IF some one should ask me to show him the place of all others which would reveal the largest number of striking flowers peculiar to the season, I should like to guide him to a certain salt-marsh —a salt-marsh which is cut up here and there by little inlets, where the water runs up at high tide and laps its way far inland, and which is dotted by occasional islands of higher, drier land that are covered with tall trees.

In the distance the marsh only looks refreshingly green, but if we draw nearer we see patches of vivid coloring for

which the bright grass of the salt-mead-
ows fails to account. If we enter it by
way of the sand-hills on the beach, we
almost hesitate to step upon the dainty
carpet which lies before us. Hundreds
of sea-pinks, or *Sabbatia*, gleam like rosy
stars above the grasses. Yet the prodigal
fashion in which this plant lavishes its
rich color upon the meadows does not
constitute its sole or even its chief claim
upon our enthusiasm, for it is as perfect
in detail as it is beautiful in the mass.
The five-parted corolla is of the purest
pink, with clear markings of red and yellow at its centre. As in the willow-herb
or fireweed, the stamens and pistils mature at different times and self-fertilization is avoided.

One peculiarly large and beautiful species is *Sabbatia chloroides*. This is found
bordering brackish ponds along the coast.
I have never been so fortunate as to see
it growing, but specimens have been sent

me from Cape Cod. A less conspicuous kind abounds in the rich soil of the interior.

Another abundant plant which is sure to excite our interest is the sea-lavender. Its small lavender - colored flowers are spiked along one side of the leafless, branching stems, giving a misty effect which makes its other common name of marsh rosemary seem peculiarly appropriate, when we know that the title is derived from the Latin for " sea-spray."

Here, too, we find the mock bishop-weed, one of the most delicate of the Parsleys, with thread-like leaves and tiny white flowers growing in bracted clusters, the shape of which might suggest to the imaginative a bishop's cap. Through this veil of flower and foliage we spy the pinkish stems, opposite, clasping leaves and small flesh-colored blossoms of the marsh St. John's-wort, an attractive plant whose chief charm, perhaps, lies in its foliage and coloring, as its flowers, although pretty, are rather small and inconspicuous.

Parts of the meadow are bright with the oblong, clover-like heads of the milkwort. These seem to deepen in color from day to day till finally they look almost red. They are closely related to the lovely fringed polygala of the June woods, and to the little moss-like species with narrow leaves growing in circles about its stem, and thick flower-heads of purplish-pink, which can be found along the inner borders of this same marsh.

There is a hollow in the meadow which is always too wet to be explored comfortably without rubber boots, and which becomes at high tide a salt-water pond. Its edges are guarded by ranks of tall swamp mallows, whose great rose-colored flowers flutter like banners in the breeze. Close by are thickets turned pinkish-purple by the dense flower - clusters of the largest and most showy of the tick - trefoils, a group of plants which are now in full bloom, and which can be recognized by their three-divided leaves, pink or purple pea-like flowers, and by the flat, roughened pods, which adhere to our clothes with regrettable pertinacity. The botany assigns this species to rich woods, but I have never seen it more abundant than here.

Only by pushing our way through a miniature-forest composed of the purple-streaked stems, divided leaves, and white flowers of another Parsley, the water-hemlock, do we reach the stretch of land which glories in the treasure which makes this especial marsh more brilliant and unusual than the many others which skirt the coast. This treasure is the yellow-fringed orchis, a plant which rears its full orange-colored domes on every side, making a mass of burning color in the morning sunlight.

I have never found an orchid growing

in such abundance elsewhere, and cannot but hope that the meadow will guard its secret, lest some wholesale despoiler should contrive to rob it permanently of its greatest beauty. Certain orchids which were abundant formerly in parts of England can no longer be found in that country, owing to the reckless fashion in which the plants, for various purposes, were uprooted and carried off. It is well, too, to remember that plucking all of its flowers is equivalent to uprooting the plant in the case of annuals and biennials, as the future life of the species depends upon the seeds which the flowers set.

In clefts of the rocks which skirt the inlet the bright scarlet petals of the pimpernel, the "poor man's weather-glass" of the English, open in the sunlight and close at the approach of a storm. The sandy bog beyond is yellow with the fragrant helmet-like flowers of the horned bladderwort.

Where the ground grows less yielding, along the borders of the tree-covered
island, are bright patches of meadow-
beauty, or *Rhexia*, a delicate, pretty
flower, with four large rounded petals of
deep purple-pink, and with pistil and stamens which protrude noticeably. Under
the trees the only conspicuous plant is the
false foxglove, with tall branches covered
with large, showy, yellow flowers, the
shape of which recalls the beautiful purple
foxglove of English lanes.

In the swamps farther inland the close
white heads of the button - bush yield a
jasmine - like fragrance. From grassy
hummocks nod the violet-purple blossoms ·
of the monkey-flower. The path of the
slow stream is defined by the bright
arrow-shaped leaves and spotless gold-
centred flowers of the arrow - head.
About the upper part of their stems are
clustered the male blossoms, their three
snowy petals surrounding the yellow sta-

mens, the rather ugly female flowers with
their dull green centres occupying a less
conspicuous position below. This is only in some cases, however ; at times the
staminate and pistillate blossoms are
found on separate plants.

The edges of the pond are blue with the
long, close spikes of the pickerel - weed.
Over the thickets on its shore the clematis
has flung a veil of feathery white. A tan-
gle of golden threads with little bunched
white flowers show that the dodder is at
its old game of living on its more self-re-
liant neighbors. From erect, finger-like
clusters comes the sweet, spicy breath of
the *Clethra*.

Where the white dust of the road pow-
ders the wayside plants rise the coarse
stalks of the evening primrose. These are
hung with faded-looking flowers whose
unsuspectedly fragrant petals gleamed
through the moonlit darkness of last
night. Among them we find a fragile,

canary-yellow blossom which has been unable to close because the pink night-moth, which is the plant's regular visitor, is so overcome with sleep, or so drunk, perhaps, with nectar, that it is quite oblivious of the growing day and of its host's custom of closing its doors with sunrise. We are so unused to seeing these gay creatures that we feel a little as if we had surprised some ballroom beauty fast asleep on the scene of her midnight triumphs.

The slender spikes of the tall purple vervain have a somewhat jagged appearance, owing to the reluctance of its little deep-hued flowers to open simultaneously. The mullein is not without this same peculiarity. Its sleepy-looking blossoms open one by one, giving the dense spike an unfinished, sluggish aspect. In fact, I think it is the most "logy" looking plant we have. Although it came to us originally from England, it is now comparatively rare in that country. Mr. Burroughs quotes a London correspondent, who says that when one comes up in solitary glory its appearance is heralded much as if it were a comet, the development of its woolly leaves and the growth of its spike being watched and reported upon day by day.

The broad, butterfly-shaped flowers of the moth-mullein, another emigrant, are much more pleasing than those of its kinsman. Their corollas are sometimes white, sometimes yellow, with a dash of red or purple at the centre. Their stamens are loaded with orange - colored pollen and bearded with tufts of violet wool, which we fancy shields some hidden nectar, as their whole appearance suggests that they aim to attract insect visitors.

Despite the aversion with which it is regarded by the farmers, and the carelessness with which it is overlooked by those who value only the unusual, the wild carrot is one of the most beautiful of our naturalized plants. There is a delicacy and symmetry in the feathery clusters suggestive of cobwebs, of magnified snowflakes, of the finest of laces (one of its common names is Queen Anne's lace), of the daintiest creations in the worlds of both art and nature.

Perhaps the most omnipresent flower just now is the yarrow. Its finely dissected leaves and close white clusters border every roadside. Indeed, when passing through New York a short time ago it showed its familiar face in a Fifth Avenue door-yard. Despite what seems to me an obvious unlikeness, it is confused frequently with the wild carrot. Five minutes' study of the two plants with a common magnifying glass will fix firmly in the mind the difference between them. It requires little botanical knowledge to recognize at once that the wild carrot is a member of the umbelliferous Parsley family. But the small heads of the yarrow so perfectly simulate separate flowers that this plant is less readily identified as a Composite.

Huddled in hollows by the roadside are the tall stout stalks, clasping woolly leaves, and great yellow disks of the elecampane, another Composite. Still another, which is never found far from the highway, is the chicory, the charm of whose sky-blue flowers is somewhat decreased by the bedraggled appearance of the rest of the plant.

Every true-born American ought to recognize the opposite, widely spreading leaves, and dull, whitish flower-clusters of the boneset, a plant which cured, or which was supposed to cure, so many of the ailments of our forefathers. Even to-day the country children eye it ruefully as it hangs in long dried bunches in the attic, waiting to be brewed at the slightest warning into a singularly nauseating draught.

Nearly related to the boneset proper

is the Joe-Pye-weed, with tall stout stems surrounded by circles of rough oblong leaves, and with intensely purple-pink flowers, which are massing themselves effectively in the low meadows. In parts of the country no plant does more for the beauty of the landscape of late summer. It is said to have taken its name from an Indian medicine-man, who found it a cure for typhus fever.

The European bellflower has become naturalized in New England, and the roadsides now are bright with its graceful lilac-blue spires. Another brilliant emigrant which is blossoming at present is the purple loosestrife. The botany extends its range from Nova Scotia to Delaware, but I find its myriad deep-hued wands only on the swampy shores of the Hudson, and in the marshes which have for their background the level outline of the Shawangunk Mountains.

Along shaded streams the jewel-weeds

hang their spurred, delicate pockets; these are sometimes pale yellow, again deep orange, spotted with reddish-brown. In certain swampy woods and open marshes we at last discover the feathery pink-purple spikes of the smaller fringed orchis.

Summer seems well advanced when the curved leafy stems of the Solomon's seal and twisted-stalk are hung, the first with blackish, the second with bright red berries. Except in the open fields fruits now are more conspicuous than flowers. Of the latter, in the woods, we note chiefly the pink blossoms strung upon the long leafless stalks of the tick-trefoil; also a somewhat similar-looking plant, the lopseed, whose small pink flowers are not pealike, however, and whose leaves are not divided, as are those of the trefoils. The inconspicuous, two-petalled blossoms and thin opposite leaves of the uninteresting enchanter's nightshade are abundant everywhere.

On the hillside the velvety crimson plumes of the staghorn sumach toss upward in the pride of fruition. Here the soft cushion of the pasture thistle yields a pleasant fragrance, and violet patches are made in the grass by the incomplete heads of the self-heal. Against the dark oval leaves of the cockspur-thorn lie red-cheeked, apple-like fruit. Currant-like clusters of choke-cherries hang from the thicket. The birds are twittering with joy at the feast which the black-cap bushes are yielding, and a song-sparrow flies to the top of a red-osier dogwood, which is heavy with its burden of white berries, and gives vent to a few bubbling notes with an ecstatic energy which threatens almost to burst its little body.

VII

Late August and Early September

Along the roadside, like the flowers of gold
That tawny Incas for their gardens wrought,
Heavy with sunshine droops the golden-rod,
And the red pennons of the cardinal-flower
Hang motionless upon their upright staves.

—WHITTIER.

VII

Late August and Early September

IN an interesting article on "American Wild Flowers" which appeared in *The Fortnightly Review* some two years ago, the English naturalist, Mr. Alfred Wallace, commented upon the fact, or what seemed to him the fact, that nowhere in our country could be seen any such brilliant masses of flowers as are yearly displayed by the moors and meadows of Great Britain.

I have not the article with me and do not recall certainly whether Mr. Wallace saw our fields and hillsides in their September dress, but I do remember that he dwelt chiefly upon our earlier flowers, and while, of course, he alluded to the many species of golden-rods and asters to be found in the United States, it seems to me quite impossible that he could have seen our country at this season and yet have remained unconvinced of the unusual brilliancy of its flora.

Despite the beauty of our woods and meadows when starred with the white of bloodroot and anemone, and with the deep red of the wake-robin, they are perhaps less radiant than those of England " in primrose-time." And although our summer landscape glows with deep-hued lilies and milkweeds, and glitters with black-eyed Susans, yet in actual brilliancy it must yield the palm to an English field of scarlet poppies. But when September lines the roadsides of New England with the purple of the aster, and flings its mantle of golden-rod over her hills, and fills her hollows with the pink drifts of the Joe-Pye-weed, or with the intense red-purple of the iron-weed, and guards her brooks with tall ranks of yellow sun-flowers, then, I think, that any moor or meadow of Great Britain might be set in her midst and yet fail to pale her glory.

Of the hundred or so classified species of golden - rod, about eighty belong to the United States. Of these some forty can be found in our Northeastern States. The scientific name of the genus, *Soli-dago*, signifying " to make whole," refers to the faith which formerly prevailed in its healing powers. It belongs to the Composite family, which now predomi-nates so generally. Its small heads are composed of both ray- and disk- flowers, which are of the same golden hue, except in one species. These flower-heads are usually clustered in one-sided racemes, which spring from the upper part of a leafy stem.

One of the commonest species, and one of the earliest to blossom, is the rough golden - rod, a plant with hairy stem, thick, rough, oblong leaves, and small heads, each one of which is made up of from seven to nine ray-flowers and from four to seven disk-flowers. Occasionally it will be found growing to a height of five or six feet, but ordinarily it is one of the lowest of the genus. The elm-leaved species is a somewhat similar-looking plant, with thinner, larger leaves, a smooth stem, and with only about four ray-flowers to each little head. The so-called Canadian golden-rod, with its tall, stout stem, pointed, sharply toothed leaves and short ray-flowers is one of the commonest varieties.

The lance-leaved species is seldom recognized as a member of the tribe because of its flat-topped clusters, which form a striking contrast to the slender, wand-like racemes which usually characterize the genus. It is often mistaken for the tansy, which is also a yellow Composite, but which is quite dissimilar in detail, having deeply divided leaves, the segments of which are cut and toothed, and sometimes much crisped or curled, and button-like, deep-hued flower-heads, which appear to be devoid of ray-flowers. Strictly speaking, the tansy is not a wild flower with us. It was brought from Europe to the gardens of New England, where it was raised as a valuable herb. Now it dyes yellow the hollows of the abandoned homestead and strays lawlessly to the borders of the highway.

The tribe of asters is even larger than that of golden-rods, numbering some two hundred species. Italy, Switzerland, and Great Britain each yield but one native variety, I believe, although others are largely cultivated; the Christmas and Michaelmas daisies of English gardens being American asters. One species,

Aster glacialis of the botanies, is found growing 12,000 feet above the sea. The blue and purple varieties, those having blue and purple ray-flowers, that is, are much commoner than those with white ray-flowers. Over fifty of the former are found in the Northeastern States to about a dozen of the latter.

Of the white species the earliest to bloom is the corymbed aster, which can be identified by its slender, somewhat zigzag stems, its thin heart-shaped leaves, and its loosely clustered flower-heads. It grows plentifully in the open woods, especially somewhat northward. In swamps and moist thickets we find the umbelled aster, with its long, tapering leaves, and flat clusters which it lifts at times to a height of seven feet. A beautiful variety which is abundant along the coast is the many - flowered aster. This is a bushy, spreading plant somewhat suggestive of an evergreen, with little, narrow, rigid leaves and small, crowded flower-heads.

The tall, stout stems and large violet heads of the New England aster mark one of the most striking of the purple species. It floods with color the low meadows and moist hollows along the roadside, while the wood - borders are lightened by the pale blue rays of the heart-leaved variety.

There are many other species without English titles which can hardly be described without the aid of technical terms. Even the trained botanist finds himself daunted at times in his efforts to identify the various species, while the beginner is sure to be sorely tried if he set himself this task. Yet if he persevere he will be rewarded, as every roadside will supply an absorbing problem : for there is a decided fascination in detecting the individual traits of plants that to the untrained eye have nothing to distinguish them from one another. The significance of the scientific title of the genus *Aster* is easily appreciated, for the effect of its flowers is peculiarly star-like.

The red - purple clusters of the iron-weed are often mistaken for asters by those who are not sufficiently observant to notice that its flower-heads are composed entirely of tubular blossoms, being without the ray-flowers which are essential to an aster. In the iron-weed the involucre of little leaf-like scales which always surrounds the flower - head of a Composite, and which is commonly considered a calyx by the unbotanical, is usually of a purplish tint, each little scale being tipped with a tiny cusp or point. Its alternate leaves are long and narrow, and its tough stem is responsible for its common name. Its scientific title, *Vernonia*, was bestowed in honor of an English botanist who travelled in this country many years ago.

In the rich woods the flat-topped flower

clusters and broad, pointed leaves of the white snakeroot, a near relative of the boneset, are noticeable. This is a brighter-looking, more ornamental plant than its celebrated kinsman. Along the streams and in the thickets the sunflowers lift their yellow heads far above our own, while the wet ditches are gilded with the bright rays of the bur-marigold.

Somewhat southward the large heads of the so-called golden aster (which is not an aster at all) star the dry fields and roadsides. In moist, shaded spots we find the ephemeral day-flower, or *Commelina*, with its two sky-blue petals quaintly commemorating the two Commelyns, distinguished Dutch botanists, while the odd petal, which can boast little in the way of either size or color, immortalizes the comparative insignificance of a less renowned brother! At least so runs the tradition.

From barren sandy banks in much the same latitudes, spring the branching stems, opposite aromatic leaves, and clustered, delicate white or lavender-colored flowers of the dittany, one of the Mints. On the hill-side the little corollas of the blue-curls are falling so as to reveal within the calyx the four tiny nutlets, which are a prominent characteristic of the same family, while the plant's clammy, balsam-scented leaves offer another means of identification.

Near the blue-curls we are likely to find the closely spiked, pea-like blossoms and three-divided leaves of the bush-clover, as well as the pink-purple flowers and downy and also clover-like foliage of another of the tick-trefoils. As these two groups of plants have so many points in common that it is somewhat difficult ordinarily to distinguish between them, it is well to remember that the calyx of a tick-trefoil is usually more or less two-lipped, while that of a bush-clover is divided into five slender and nearly equal lobes.

Two other members of the Pulse or Pea

family are frequently encountered during the earlier part of this month. Along the grassy lanes that wind in and out among the woods are delicate clusters of pale lilac blossoms nodding from a stem which clambers over the thicket and twines about the iron-weeds and asters. I believe this graceful plant owes its unattractive name of hogpeanut to its subterranean fruit, which is said to be uprooted and devoured by hogs. In low places, climbing about whatever shrub or plant it chances to find, grows the wild bean, with thick clusters of brown and pinkish flowers which yield a delicate fragrance somewhat suggestive of violets. My experience has been that these four members of the Pulse family are especially abundant along the coast.

The salt meadows are bright with the purplish-pink shells of the seaside gerardia. These flowers, although smaller, are almost identical in shape with those of their relative, the yellow false foxglove, which we found in the woods some time ago. The slender gerardia is a similar-looking plant which abounds farther inland. This genus is named after the early botanist, Gerarde, author of the famous " Herball." Its members are supposed to be more or less parasitic in their habits, drawing their nourishment from the roots of other plants. For some time the pale foliage of the salt-marsh fleabane has been conspicuous by contrast among the daily deepening flower-heads of the milkwort and the bright green leaves of the marsh St. John's-wort, and finally it spreads before us its pink clusters of tiny, strongly scented flowers.

Some weeks since I described the pick-erel-weed and arrow - head as in their prime, but it must be remembered that a plant which flowers in August in Southern New York and New Jersey may not blos-som in the mountains farther north until September. Along the Saranac River in the Adirondacks a few days ago I found

the pickerel-weed more fully and luxuri-
antly in bloom than on any previous occasion. The slender spikes of delicate
blue flowers reared themselves above great
beds of dark, polished leaves, making a
rich border to the winding river. Our
guide told us that in spring the pickerel
laid their eggs among these plants, which
at that season are not visible above the
water, and that later the moose fed upon
their leaves.

The shoals were still starred with the
pure blossoms of the arrow-head, while in
the current of the stream trembled the
thick pink spikes of the amphibious knotweed. At the foot of the rush-like
leaves and golden-brown spires of the
cat-tail, and among the soft round heads
of the bur-reed, protruded the knobby
buds and coarse bright flowers of the yellow pond-lily. In places where the logs
sent down the river the previous winters
had ''jammed,'' the fuzzy whitish pyra-

mids of the meadow-sweet spired upward by the hundred.

On the banks the blossoms of the fire-weed had made way for the pink, slender pods which were about to crack open, releasing cloudy masses of silver-winged seeds. Great clusters of delicate *Osmunda* ferns leaned over the water's edge. The tall stems and white, huddled flowers of the turtle-head hardly succeeded in keeping out of the stream. As a dark curve of shore swept in sight, against its background of spruce, birch, and hemlock, gleamed

> " The cardinal and the blood-red spots,
> Its double in the stream."

In this flower seems to culminate the vivid beauty of the summer. Yet, despite its intense color, it is so sure to choose a cool, rich setting that it never suggests heat, as do the field flowers of the earlier year.

Many of the lily pads had been turned over by the swift current, or perhaps by a passing boat, and showed the deep, polished pink of their lower sides. Thick among them floated their placid, queenly flowers, with their green and pink-tinged sepals, and their snowy petals which pass imperceptibly into the centre of golden stamens. The bright red twigs of the dogwood, the coral clusters of the now beautiful hobble-bush and a stray branch of crimson maple lightened the more thickly wooded banks.

As we left the boat, stepping upon the elastic carpet of moss and pine-needles and crossing a fallen, lichen-grown tree trunk, we discovered the low white flower and violet-like leaves of the *Dalibarda*, and were filled with wonder and delight when we found the pink, fragrant bells of the *Linnæa* still heralding the fame of their great master. The tiny, evergreen, birch-flavored leaves of the creeping snowberry almost hid from view its spotless fruit, but the peculiarly bright blue berries of the

Clintonia were everywhere conspicuous as they rose above their large polished leaves. Among delicate masses of the clover-like foliage of the wood - sorrel lurked a late pink - veined blossom. And where we looked only for gleaming clusters of scarlet fruit we found the white, petal-like leaves of the bunchberry. If in June we were saddened by the first transmutations of flower into fruit, apparent symbols of a year that is no longer young, in September we are compensated by these unexpected emblems of its eternal youth.

VIII

Autumn

Oh, sacrament of summer days,
Oh, last communion in the haze,
Permit a child to join,

Thy sacred emblems to partake,
Thy consecrated bread to break,
Taste thine immortal wine!
                    —EMILY DICKINSON.

VIII

Autumn

ON every perfect day, Nature, like a beautiful woman, cajoles her true lovers into the belief that she has never before worn so becoming a dress. I have a conviction of long standing that the world is fairest when the trees are first laced with green, and little tender things are pushing up everywhere and bursting into miracles of delicate bloom. Yet, with each heaven-born morning of the succeeding seasons, this somewhat spasmodic faith is weakly surrendered. It is impossible to wonder at Lowell's

" What is so rare as a day in June ? "

when the lanes are first lined with white-flowered shrubs, and the air is heavy with fragrance and alive with bird - voices. Later, without one backward glance, I abandon myself to the ripe, luscious beauty of midsummer. And though, while taking my first fall walk the other day (for the true fall is not here till well on in September), and while noting how the hills were veiled by a silvery mist, and how the roadsides wore a many-hued embroidery, and that the sumach in the swamp was beginning to look like the burning bush on Horeb, I felt that there could be no beauty like this, which foretold the end; yet already I realize that before long the purple shadows will lie so softly upon the snowy fields, and the faint rose of dawn or twilight will flush with such tenderness the white side of the mountain, that the earth may seem lovelier in her shroud than in any of her living garments.

But it is altogether human to set especial value upon the things of which we
are about to be deprived, and now, more
than ever, we linger out of doors, yielding ourselves to influences which lie upon
our spirits like a benediction, storing our
minds with images which, among less in-
spiring surroundings, will

> —— "flash upon that inward eye,
> Which is the bliss of solitude."

Few flowers are abroad, barring the asters
and golden-rods, yet these few we invest
with a peculiar interest and affection, ex-
periencing a sensation of gratitude, almost, as toward some beings who have
stood stanch when the multitudes fell
away.

No group of plants belong more distinc-
tively to the season than do the gentians.
Of these, the most famous, though by no
means the most frequent representative, is
the fringed gentian, a flower which owes,

I fancy, much of its reputation to Bryant's well-known lines ; not that it does
not deserve the interest which has centred about it, but that, while everyone
has heard of it, comparatively few people
seem to have ferreted out its haunts.
Probably Bryant, also, is largely responsible for the somewhat inaccurate notions
which are afloat concerning its usual season of blooming.   This is in September,
long before the

——"woods are bare and birds are flown " ;

although Thoreau, if I remember rightly,
records that he found it in flower as late
as November 7th, when certainly,

> ——"frosts and shortening days portend
> The aged year is near his end."

My first fringed gentian was the re-
ward of a forty-mile drive, taken one
cold autumn day for the sole purpose of
paying court to its blue loveliness.   It
enticed us into a wet, green meadow,

where, picking our way from hummock to hummock, without appreciably diminishing the supply, we gathered one tall cluster after another of the delicate, deep-hued blossoms. In bud the fringed petals are twisted one about the other. When the day is cloudy, or even, I should judge, if the wind is high, the full-blown flower closes in the same fashion. The individuals which grow in the shade are even more attractive than those which frequent the open. Their blue is lighter, with a silvery tinge which I do not recall in any other flower. Until this year I have never encountered the plant in my ordinary wanderings, but during the past few days I have found it bordering in abundance the Berkshire lanes. Being a biennial, we cannot predict with certainty its whereabouts from year to year, as its seeds may be washed to some distance in the moist regions which usually it favors.

Far less delicate and uncommon, but still attractive, is the closed gentian. This is usually a stout, rather tall plant, with crowded clusters of deep blue or purple flowers, which never open, looking always like buds. It grows along the shaded roadsides, and is easily confused with other members of the group, as both the five-flowered and soapwort gentians have narrow corollas, which often appear almost closed.

Certain New England woods and roadsides are now tinged with the pale blue or at times pinkish blossoms of the five-flowered species, while in the Adirondacks in early September, parts of the shore of the Raquette River were actually " blued " with what I take to have been the lance-leaved gentian, *Gentiana linearis* of the botany, formerly considered a variety of the soapwort species. This conjecture as to their identity was never verified, as the specimens gathered for analysis were thrown away by the guide during a storm which overtook us on one of the "carries."

In the wet meadows which harbor the fringed gentian we find also the white or cream-colored flowers of the grass of Parnassus, their five veiny petals crowning a tall, slender stem, which is clasped below by a little rounded leaf. There is a suggestion of spring in a fresh cluster of these blossoms, perhaps owing to a superficial resemblance to the anemones, or it may be because they have little of the hardy look of other fall flowers.

Here, too, abounds the last orchid of the year, the ladies' tresses, with small white flowers growing in a slender twisted spike. Occasionally this plant becomes ambitious. Leaving the low, "wet places" to which it is assigned by the botany, it climbs far up the hillsides. I never remember seeing it in greater abundance, or more fragrant and perfect, than in a field high up on the Catskill Mountains. The flowers that we care for we are apt to associate with the particular spot in which we found them first—or at their best—and the mention or sight of this little orchid instantly recalls that breezy upland with its far-reaching view, and its hum of eager bees which were sucking the rare sweets of the late year from the myriad spires among which I lay one September morning.

Another plant linked for me with the same region and season is the so-called Canadian violet. Till late September, along a winding mountain road, one could gather great bunches of its fresh, leafy - stemmed flowers — white, yellow-centred, fragrant, with purple veins above and violet - washed below. Near them the wild strawberries were abundantly in blossom, as they are now to some extent in Berkshire.

And whenever I see a depauperate

mountain-ash forlornly decorating a corner of some over-civilized country-place, languishing like a handsome young barbarian in captivity, I remember how that same road brought one to the forest which crowned the mountain's top—to a dimly lighted path which led through mossy fern-beds, till it reached a sudden opening, where two great hemlocks made a frame, and a dark, distant mountain formed a background for the feathery foliage and scarlet clusters of a superbly vigorous specimen of this beautiful tree.

If we leave the mountains and visit once more the salt meadows we notice a multitude of erect narrow-leaved stems, which toward their summits are studded with soft, rose-purple flowerheads. This is the blazing star, one of the latest blooming and most beautiful of the Composites.

Just back of the beach the gray sand-hills are warm with the slender branches and little rose-colored flowers of the sand knotweed, a patch of which reminded Thoreau of "a peach orchard in bloom." The bright-hued, leafless stems of the glasswort define the borders of the road. Only a close examination convinces us of the existence of the minute flowers of this odd-looking plant, for they are so sunken in its thickened upper joints as to be almost invisible.

Now and then we come across an evening primrose with blossoms so wide open, delicate and fragrant, and with leaf and stem so lacking their usual rankness, that we can hardly connect it with the great, coarse plants whose brown, flowerless spikes are crowding the edge of the highway. In this neighborhood the brilliant flowers and fleshy leaves of the seaside golden-rod are everywhere conspicuous, while farther inland the so-called blue-stemmed species, bearing its clustered heads in the leaf-angles along the stem, begins to predominate. On the moun-

tains and in the dry thickets of the low-
lands we encounter occasionally one of
the most attractive of the tribe—the sweet
golden-rod, with shining, dotted, narrow
leaves, which yield, when crushed, a refreshing anise-like odor.

The different asters are affording the
loveliest shades of blue, purple, and lavender.   Pre-eminent for richness of color
and beauty of detail are the large, violet-
hued, daisy-like heads of the showy aster,
a species which is found growing in sandy
soil along the coast.   In the woods, nodding from tall stems, we notice the graceful, bell-like flower-heads of the rattle-
snake-root.

A friend writes me that in parts of Connecticut the swamps are still bright with
the great blue lobelia, and that the yellow
flowers of the bur-marigold are abundant
in the roadside ditches.   This last-named
plant holds its own through the first frosts
till well on in November.   Its dull-look-

ing sister, the common stick-tight, whose ugly brownish flower-heads are frequent in moist, waste places, is equally tenacious of life—and of our clothes, to which its barbed seed-vessels cling so persistently that every walk across country means that we have innocently extended its unwelcome sway.

Indeed, we can hardly spend a morning out of doors at this season without having our attention drawn constantly to the many ingenious devices adopted by the different plants for the distribution of their seed. On ourselves and on our dogs we find not only the troublesome barbs of the stick-tight, but also the flat, hooked pods of the tick-trefoils, the bristly fruit of avens and goose-grass, and the prickly heads of the burdock. In the thicket the birds are already stripping the dogwoods of their red, blue, and lead-colored berries, either releasing the seeds upon the spot or carrying them to some other and perhaps more hospitable neighborhood. While the coral beads of the beautiful black alder, the red or purple sprays of the viburnums, the bright haws of the white-thorn, the scarlet pennants which stream from the barberry bushes, and the half-hidden berries of the partridge-vine, tempt them to a feast which will prove as advantageous to host as to guest.

If the seeds are not trapped out in a fashion which renders them attractive to animals their transportation generally is provided in some other manner. Notice how the great pasture thistle is slowly swelling into a silvery cushion which a few brisk winds will disintegrate. Watch the pods of the milkweed crack open, revealing symmetrical packs (the beloved "fishes" of childhood) of golden-brown seeds, to each one of which is tacked a silky sail which finally unfurls and floats away with its burden. Go down to the brook and finger lightly the pod of the jewel-weed, or touch-me-not. You will become so fascinated with the ingenious mechanism which causes the little seed-vessel to recoil from your touch with an elastic spring which sends the seeds far into the neighboring thicket, that you will hardly leave till the last tiny advent-urer has been started on his life-journey.

On the hillside grows a shrub with wavy-toothed leaves, and a nut-like fruit which has been ripening all summer. We know that this is the witch-hazel, because little bunches of fragrant, narrow-petalled yellow flowers are bursting from the branches. All the blossoms may not ap-pear for some time yet, but when the fruit has ripened and the leaves are fallen they will surprise us like a golden prophecy of spring. Break off and carry home a fruit-ing branch. Soon the capsules will snap elastically apart, discharging in every di-rection their black, bony contents; the action of the parent plant somewhat recalling that of the mother bird who pushes her young from the edge of the nest that they may learn to shift for themselves.

Many seeds are washed by water to more or less remote neighborhoods. Some become attached with clods of earth to the feet of birds, and are borne to other regions, where they thrive or perish, according to their power of adapting themselves to their new environment. How far this last class of travellers may journey we realize especially at this season, when nearly every day shows us fresh flocks of birds which have come under the influence of that strange power which moves them "to stretch their wings toward the South," bringing them (even the more timid species) this morning to our very doorstep in search of food, inducing them to-night to resume a voyage which may terminate only in the tropics.

Each walk abroad brings up new questions for settlement. The last is one of preference pure and simple, namely, whether the ''snake'' fence or the stone wall affords the greater possibilities. Till recently I had no doubt as to the æsthetic superiority of the stone wall. It has such infinite capacity for tumbling, for taking on a coat of lichens and mosses, —for wearing soft tints of time and weather. When quite prostrate its ruin is hidden so tenderly by blood-red tangles of Virginia creeper, or silky plumes of clematis, and by masses of soft ferns, which nestle lovingly about its feet. In the presence of the ideal stone wall, and I know a hundred such, there seems no room for indecision.

Yet the crooked course of the ''snake'' fence is undeniably picturesque. Its '' zigzags '' offer singularly choice retreats for great clumps of purple-stalked, red-stained, heavy-fruited poke-weed, for groups of yellow-brown *Osmunda* ferns, and for festoons of bitter-sweet, with orange pods split open to reveal their scarlet-coated seeds. No stone wall can yield such occasional vistas of meadow beyond, bright with golden-rod and aster, and framed by brilliant strands of black-berry vine. When its plants and shrubs and creepers are left quite unmolested, free to follow its devious course, to twine about its posts, or to peep confidingly over its topmost rails, then, I own, my loyalty begins to waver.

But after a time the rambler out of doors grows accustomed to leaving his questions unanswered. Plant-nature, es-pecially, he finds almost as inconsistent and contradictory as his own. Surprises soon cease to be surprising. Even now the rank stems of the chicory are studded with bright blue blossoms. The sun shines warm and sweet upon grass which is green and tender as in June. Sooth-ing insect - murmurs so fill the air that the absence of bird-notes is hardly felt.

Clover - heads are full and deep - hued, yielding stores of nectar to the bees. All about are bright groups of black-eyed Susan—a plant which two months ago looked brown and "done for." Feathery clusters of wild carrot (reminding Walt Whitman of "delicate pats of snowflakes") spread themselves beside the fruiting umbels, which look like collapsed birds'-nests. Daisies are fresh, and buttercups so glossy that one can hardly resist brushing them with his lips to see if they are actually wet.

Yet the maple which leans clear across the brook is already crimson, and when we reach the rocky hillside the yellow fronds of the *Dicksonia* exhale a subtle fragrance which suggests decay. Another faint, elusive odor, starting a train of equally elusive memories, floats upward from the only flower at our feet, the "life-everlasting," which, as children, I hardly know why, we always associated with graves. Here,

where there is none of the life and freshness of the meadow below, it seems to
decorate the grave of summer.   Dr.
Holmes says concerning it: "A something it has of sepulchral spicery, as if it
had been brought from the core of some
great pyramid, where it had lain on the
breast of a mummied Pharaoh. Something, too, of immortality in the sad,
faint sweetness lingering long in its life-
less petals.   Yet this does not tell why it
fills my eyes with tears, and carries me in
blissful thought to the banks of asphodel
that border the River of Life."

Index

PAGE

Adder's mouth, ... 84
Adder's tongue, ... 27, 28
Alders, ... 20
Alder, black, ... 143
Anemone, ... 25
Anemone, summer, ... 87
Anemones, ... 30
Arbutus, trailing, ... 25
Arrow-head, ... 101, 125
Ash, mountain, ... 139
Aster, golden, ... 121
Asters, ... 72, 114, 117, 133, 141
Avens, ... 142
Azalea, wild, ... 33, 43

Baneberry, ... 34, 86
Barbara, St., herb of, ... 37
Barberry, ... 143
Beach-pea, ... 82
Bean, wild, ... 123
Beech, ... 23
Bellflower, ... 107
Bellwort, ... 30
Birches, ... 23
Bishop-weed, mock, ... 97
Bitter-sweet, ... 146
Blackberry-vine, ... 66, 147
Black-cap bushes, ... 109
Black-eyed Susan, ... 72, 140
Bladder campion, ... 87
Bladderwort, horned, ... 100
Blazing star, ... 139
Bloodroot, ... 25

Index

	PAGE
Blue-curls,	122
Blue-eyed grass,	35, 55
Bluets,	44
Boneset,	106
Buckbean,	44
Bugbane,	85
Bunch-berry,	60, 128
Burdock,	142
Bur-marigold,	121, 141
Bur-reed,	125
Bush-clover,	122
Bush-honeysuckle,	86
Buttercups,	45, 55, 148
Butterfly-weed,	76
Button-bush,	101
Cabbage, skunk,	43
Calopogon,	83
Campion, bladder,	87
Cardinal-flower,	126
Carrion-vine,	58
Carrot, wild,	104, 148
Cat-brier,	58
Cat-tail,	125
Celandine,	36
Chicory,	106
Choke-cherries,	109
Cinquefoil,	36
Clematis,	102, 146
Clethra,	102
Clintonia,	41, 128
Clover,	50
Clover, bush,	122
Clover-heads,	148
Clover, yellow hop	53
Cockle, corn,	90
Cockspur-thorn,	109
Cohosh, black,	85
Columbine,	29

PAGE

Commelina, ... 121
Composite family, ... 72, 74
Cone-flower, ... 73
Cornel, dwarf, ... 60
Corpse-plant, ... 86
Cranesbill, wild, ... 39
Cruciferæ, ... 37
Cynthia, ... 38

Daisies, ... 45, 55, 72, 148
Daisies, Michaelmas, ... 117
Daisy, ... 73, 74
Dalibarda, ... 127
Dandelion, ... 45, 73
Day-flower, ... 141
Dicksonia, ... 148
Dittany, ... 122
Dodder, ... 102
Dogbane, ... 89
Dogwood, ... 33, 43, 60, 127
Dogwood, red-osier, ... 109
Dogwoods, ... 142
Dutchman's breeches, ... 27

Elder, ... 82
Elder, early, ... 86
Elder, red-berried, ... 33
Elecampane, ... 106
Elms, ... 22
Enchanter's nightshade, ... 108
Evening primrose, ... 102
Evening primrose, day-blooming, ... 55

Fern, cinnamon, ... 43
Fern, royal, ... 42
Fireweed 88, 126
Flag, blue, ... 35, 55
Fleabane, salt-marsh, ... 124
Fleur-de-lis, ... 35
Foam-flower, ... 34

PAGE

Forget-me-nots, ... 45
Foxglove, false, ... 101, 123

Gentian, closed, ... 136
Gentian, fringed, ... 133
Gentian, five-flowered, ... 136
Gentian, lance-leaved, ... 136
Gentian, soapwort, ... 136
Gentiana linearis, ... 136
Geranium, wild, ... 38
Gerardia, seaside, ... 123
Gerardia, slender, ... 124
Ginger, wild, ... 29
Ginseng, dwarf, ... 30
Glasswort, ... 140
Golden-rod, ... 115, 140, 141
Gold-thread, ... 41
Goose-grass, ... 142
Grape, wild, ... 58
Grass-pink, ... 83
Grass of Parnassus, ... 137

Hellebore, false, ... 25, 43, 58, 83
Hemlock, water, ... 89, 99
Herb of St. Barbara, ... 37
Hobble-bush, ... 127
Hog-peanut, ... 123
Honeysuckle, bush, ... 86
Honeysuckle, white swamp, ... 82
Hop-clover, yellow, ... 53

Indian cucumber-root, ... 63
Indian moccason, ... 40
Indian pipe, ... 86
Indigo, wild, ... 85
Iron-weed, ... 115, 120

Jack-in-the-pulpit, ... 34
Jewel-weed, ... 144

PAGE

Jewel-weeds, ... 107
Joe-Pye-weed,. 107, 115

Knotweed, amphibious, ... 125
Knotweed, sand, ... 140

Ladies' tresses, ... 137
Lady's slipper, ... 40
Lady's slipper, larger yellow, ... 41
Lady's slipper, smaller yellow, ... 41
Lady's slipper, showy, ... 58, 83
Lambkill, ... 63
Laurel, mountain, ... 62
Laurel, sheep, ... 6, 63
Laurestinus, ... 59
Lavender, sea, ... 97
Life-everlasting, ... 148
Lilium superbum, ... 82
Lily, meadow, ... 77
Lily, tiger, ... 81
Lily, Turk's cap, ... 86
Lily, water, ... 127
Lily, wood, ... 80
Lily, yellow pond, ... 125
Linnæa, ... 39, 127
Liverwort, ... 25, 26
Lobelia, great blue, ... 141
Loosestrife, four-leaved, ... 89
Loosestrife, purple, ... 107
Loosestrife, yellow, ... 66, 89
Lopseed, ... 108
Lupine, ... 45

Maianthemum, ... 34
Mallows, swamp, ... 98
Maple, ... 18, 21, 22, 148
Marigold, bur, ... 121, 141
Marigold, marsh, ... 26
Marsh marigold, ... 26
Marsh rosemary, ... 97

PAGE

Marsh, St. John's-wort, ... 97
May-apple, ... 35
Meadow-beauty, ... 101
Meadow-parsnip, ... 89
Meadow-parsnip, early, ... 38
Meadow-rue, tall, ... 81
Meadow-sweet, ... 124
Milkweed, ... 76, 146
Milkwort, ... 98, 123
Moccason, Indian, ... 40
Mock bishop-weed, ... 97
Monkey-flower, ... 101
Moth-mullein, ... 104
Mountain laurel, ... 62
Mullein, ... 103
Mustards, ... 37

New Jersey tea, ... 84
Nightshade, enchanter's, ... 108

Orchid, ... 7, 8, 9, 10, 40, 41, 100
Orchis, green, ... 58, 84
Orchis, purple-fringed, great, ... 42
Orchis, purple-fringed, smaller, ... 84, 108
Orchis, showy, ... 40
Orchis, white, northern, ... 84
Orchis, yellow-fringed, ... 99
Osmunda, ... 42, 126, 146

Parsley family, ... 105
Parsleys, ... 97, 99
Parsnip, early meadow, ... 38
Parsnip, meadow, ... 89
Partridge vine, ... 64, 143
Pea, beach, ... 82
Peanut, hog, ... 123
Pickerel weed, ... 102, 125
Pimpernel, ... 100
Pink, grass, ... 83
Pink, sea, ... 96

PAGE

Pipsissewa, ... 61
Pitcher plant, ... 44
Poison ivy, ... 59
Poke-weed, ... 146
Polygala, fringed, ... 8, 40
Polypodium, ... 27
Pond lily, yellow, ... 125
Poor man's weather-glass, ... 100
Primrose, evening, ... 102, 140
Primrose, blooming evening, ... 55
Pulse family, ... 122
Pyrola , ... 61

Quaker-ladies, ... 44

Radish, wild, ... 90
Ragwort, golden, ... 37
Raspberry bushes, ... 88
Raspberry, purple-flowering, ... 89
Rattlesnake root, ... 141
Rattlesnake weed, ... 66
Red-root, ... 84
Reed, bur, ... 125
Rhexia, ... 101
Rhododendron. 68
Rose, wild, ... 89
Rosemary, marsh, ... 97
Rue, meadow, ... 81

Sabbatia, ... 96
St. John's-wort, ... 89
"   "   marsh, ... 97
Salt-marsh fleabane, ... 124
Saxifrage, early, ... 27
Sea-lavender, ... 97
Sea-pinks, ... 96
Self-heal, ... 109
Shad-bush, ... 25, 45
Sheep laurel, ... 63
Sheep-sorrel, ... 6, 44

Index

	PAGE
Silkweed,	76
Skullcap, larger,	66
Skunk cabbage,	43
Snakeroot, white,	121
Snowberry, creeping,	127
Solidago,	115
Solomon's seal,	34, 108
Solomon's seal, false,	34
Sorrel, sheep,	6, 44
Sorrel, wood,	60
Sorrel, wood, common,	36
Speedwell,	35
Spice-bush,	20
Spring beauty,	29
Stargrass,	44
Stick-tight,	142
Strawberries, wild,	66, 138
Sumach,	132
Sumach, staghorn,	109
Sunflowers,	115, 121
Swallow-worts,	77
Swamp mallows,	98
Tansy,	117
Tea, New Jersey,	84
Thimble-weed,	87
Thistle,	73, 109, 143
Thorn, cockspur,	109
Thorn, white,	143
Thyme, wild,	90
Tick-trefoil,	99, 108, 122, 142
Tiger-lily,	81
Touch-me-not,	144
Trailing arbutus,	25
Trefoil, tick,	99, 108, 122, 142
Trifolium incarnatum,	54
Trillium, white,	29
Trillium, painted,	29
Turtle-head,	126

PAGE

Twayblade, ... 58
Twinflower, ... 39
Twisted stalk, ... 34, 108

Umbelliferæ, ... 38

Vernonia, ... 120
Vervain, purple, ... 103
Vetch, blue, ... 82
Viburnum, ... 33, 43, 58, 59, 60, 103, 143
Violets, ... 30, 138
Virginia creeper, ... 146

Wake-robin, ... 28
Water-hemlock, ... 89, 99
Whip-poor-will's-shoe, ... 41
Whitehearts, ... 27
White-thorn, ... 143
Willow-herb, ... 88
Willows, ... 20
Winter-cress, ... 37
Wintergreen, ... 86
Witch-hazel, ... 144
Wood lily, ... 80
Wood-sorrel, ... 60
Wood-sorrel, common, ... 36

Yarrow, ... 105